TRAPPED!

Quite suddenly, the swimmer arrived. He must have been half submerged by the wave which bore him in. The five-foot wall of water broke halfway up the stony bank. Its foam licked up and up, to within a yard of where Sven stood. Then, defeated, the water went back, taking gravel with it and filling the air again with the grinding chatter.

In that moment Sven saw the swimmer. He was on all fours, with water and stones slithering past him. It was the moment Sven had waited for. This was the time for a quick rush forward. He had already planned what he would do. He would slip his rope about the man's waist, locking them both together, then they would begin the climb up the bank to a spot where the next wave could not reach them.

It was all clear in Sven's mind—but he did not move. The swimmer was not his father. He was not even a member of the schooner's crew. This valiant swimmer who had defeated the great Atlantis rollers a man....

THE STRANGE INTRUDER
was originally published by Lothrop, Lee & Shepard Co., Inc.

About the Author:

ARTHUR CATHERALL enjoys exploring the unfamiliar lands and regions in which he sets his many outstanding adventure stories. In the process he has climbed mountains in Lapland and Algeria, ridden camels in the Sahara, and sailed aboard trawlers and tramp steamers in the Arctic and Atlantic. When not traveling, he makes his home in Bolton, England. Several years ago Mr. Catherall voyaged to the Faroe Islands, the locale of this story, and spent some time there, getting to know the islanders and their way of life.

THE STRANGE
INTRUDER

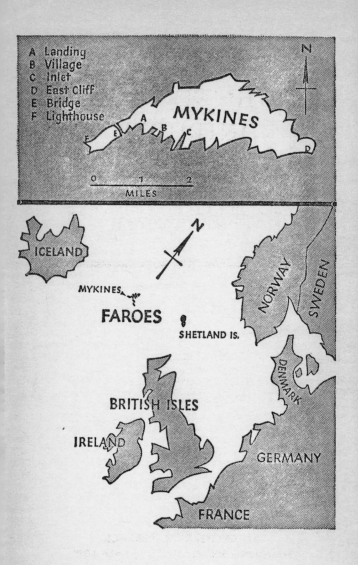

THE STRANGE
INTRUDER

(Original British title:
The Strange Invader)

———————◆———————

by Arthur Catherall

AN ARCHWAY PAPERBACK
WASHINGTON SQUARE PRESS   •   NEW YORK

THE STRANGE INTRUDER

An Archway Paperback edition

1st printing.....................September, 1968
2nd printing.....................October, 1969

Frontispiece map by Ursula Suess.

L

Published by Washington Square Press,
a division of Simon & Schuster, Inc., 630 Fifth Avenue, New York, N.Y.

WASHINGTON SQUARE PRESS editions are distributed in the
U.S. by Simon & Schuster, Inc., 630 Fifth Avenue, New
York, N.Y. 10020 and in Canada by Simon & Schuster
of Canada, Ltd., Richmond Hill, Ontario, Canada.

Standard Book Number: 671-29041-X.

Contents

THE STRANGE
INTRUDER

1: Collision!

Like a bandit waiting for a victim, the large piece of iron-bound timber lay almost hidden, with only an inch or so showing above the surface of the water. Eight months earlier it had been part of the wheelhouse of a Scottish trawler, which had gone ashore one stormy night and been pounded to pieces on one of the Faroe Islands. This chunk of wreckage, weighing several hundred pounds, had floated slowly northwest, and now lay some fifty miles distant from the tiny island of Mykines, the most westerly outpost of the lonely Faroes.

In those desolate northern waters, where the Gulf Stream meets an icy current coming down from the Polar seas, rain, mist, sunshine, and high winds can follow one another in a matter of hours. Few ships cross that part of the northern Atlantic, and it seemed as if the sodden piece of driftwood could float forever without meeting anything. Yet, like a needle drawn to a powerful magnet, a vessel was driving relentlessly toward it.

1

Aboard the 900-ton cod schooner *Faroes Seeker* everyone was happy. After a hard six months' trip up the Davis Straits, the men were looking forward to docking within twelve hours. Ahead of them was Thorshavn, capital of the Faroes. They would be paid off there and could go home.

The crew were putting the finishing touches to smartening up the ship; only the master and the mate watched the sky. The seas were unnaturally smooth; in addition the glass was falling, sure sign of imminent bad weather. There was not even a cat's-paw of wind, so the big sails hung limp. In an effort to make harbor before night fell, the diesels had been put on full throttle and were thrumming away busily.

The nearest Faroes island, little Mykines, was less than fifty miles away when the schooner's bows ground the piece of wreckage under, and rolled it along the keel.

The engineer felt the slight but unusual vibration, and looked up for a moment from his logbook in which he was making an entry.

Then, from the stern, came a series of sickening thumps as the iron-bound timber drifted into the clutches of the three-bladed screw. The helmsman was flung sideways as the brass-bound wheel spun wildly—sign that the rudder had been forced hard over.

Within moments the thumping stopped, and the

2

steady thrum-thrum-thrum of the diesels changed. The propeller shaft had snapped off, dropping the buckled screw down into the depths, and freed from its load, the diesels screamed to a speed which could only end in destruction.

Dropping his pencil and notebook, the engineer rushed for the controls, but before he could throttle back, the damage was done. From within the green-painted engine casing there came a terrifying "whump." In an instant the engine room was filled with flying pieces of metal, as deadly as shrapnel from an exploding shell.

Flames leaped high. A fractured feed pipe spurted oil for a second, and then flame. The engineer was thrown across his locker, where he lay like a broken doll.

The schooner, with blue smoke pouring from her engine-room casing windows, began to turn, for her rudder was jammed hard over. Men who had been polishing brasses dropped their rags and looked to the wheelhouse for orders as a bell began to ring, calling them to fire stations.

Half an hour later the radio operator at Thorshavn picked up a faint whisper of Morse. It was the *Faroes Seeker* calling for aid.

A telephone call to the Thorshavn harbor master's office brought the bad news that there were no vessels available, either to tow the schooner in to port or to go out to bring off the injured engineer.

The radio operator called the *Faroes Seeker*. He had earlier asked all stations and ships in the area to maintain a listening silence until he had got help for the schooner. To the master of the schooner he radioed:

"Am calling Lerwick in the Shetlands to see if Norwegian rescue ship stationed there can help. I am also asking Mykines to send a motor boat to take off your injured man. In the meantime prepare for bad weather. Weather report indicates gale force wind from northwest. Keep on the air—will call you again after I have spoken to Shetland and Mykines."

Just ten minutes later he called the *Faroes Seeker* again, to report that the Norwegian rescue ship was leaving Shetland within the hour, but would not be in the area for at least twenty hours. Mykinesholmur lighthouse keeper had been contacted and would get the Mykines islanders to put to sea. Then he asked for a report on the injured man. The Thorshavn harbor master was trying to get hold of a doctor so that medical advice could be sent by radio if need be.

There was no reply from the *Faroes Seeker*.

Even with his set boosted to the limit, the Thorshavn radio operator could get only a faint suggestion of Morse through the background hum. He called again and again, listened again and again. When he finally reported to the harbor master his voice was flat and toneless:

"Lost contact, sir, and there is a force ten gale blowing up. If the schooner's radio remains out of action I don't see how the Norwegian rescue ship can hope to find her—except by a miracle."

"Keep calling her," was the order, an order which the radio operator obeyed for hour after hour, but without success.

2: Sven's Disappointment

At the time when the *Faroes Seeker* collided with the wreckage, pale sunshine was lighting up the southern cliffs of Mykines Island. The drab olive-brown rock faces, at some places climbing six hundred feet up from the sea, were marked at irregular intervals by crude horizontal white lines which looked as though they might have been painted on the rock.

The white strips, however, kept changing. They were not paint, nor strata of white rock, but tens of thousands of sea birds. A colony of lordly gannets kept to ledges that seemed to be reserved for them alone. The other ledges housed a dozen different varieties: puffins, fulmars, kittiwakes, Manx shearwaters, arctic terns, black and white guillemots, and others.

From a fifteen-foot fishing boat heaving and rolling some eighty yards from the foot of the cliffs,

Sven Klakk stared upward. The air seemed to be filled with minute scraps of white paper, floating upward to the ledges and then shooting down to the sea. The scraps were not paper, but sea birds on a constant patrol for food.

The gannets came down on gliding wings, which would suddenly close when the bird was thirty feet above the sea. There would be a splash, a trail of bubbles beneath the surface, and a minute later the gannet would reappear with a fish in its bill.

Sven Klakk, tall and broad-shouldered for his sixteen years, was seeing none of this activity. His gaze wandered from point to point on the higher reaches of the cliffs where six men were poised precariously on ledges. With a net, rather like an over-sized butterfly-net, on the end of a fifteen-foot rod, the islanders were catching birds to use as food for the coming winter. The strange thing was that the sea birds never seemed to notice them—perhaps because their clothes blended well with the rock, or because each man had half a dozen stuffed guillemots scattered about on the ledges near him.

The air currents which swept ceaselessly along the face of the cliffs bore the hurrying throngs of birds here and there in never-ending flight, and every minute one of them would wing within reach of an islander. His slender rod would reach out in what seemed almost a casual way. There would be a grunt from the bird as it struck the netting, and

7

within twenty seconds the latest victim would be dead, and tucked by the neck in the islander's belt.

Sven's companion in the bobbing, rolling boat, a man in his early sixties, was holding a match to his pipe when Sven gave a snort of disgust.

"Uncle Aksel, did you see that?" the boy exclaimed. "That's the third in a row that Hendrik has missed. I'll bet he hasn't got half as many birds as the others. He's too old. I wouldn't miss like that if they'd give me a chance up there."

Aksel Berge tamped the glowing tobacco in his pipe bowl with the tip of a forefinger before replying. "It isn't always the man, Sven. The air currents can be tricky. I should know—I've been up there often enough."

"Well, I've been up there, haven't I?" Sven said impatiently, "only they'll not let me use the *fleyg* (the fowling net). I'm good enough on the cliff to get eggs, but not birds. I think it's stupid not letting people go for birds until they are seventeen. What difference is there between sixteen and seventeen?"

"A year!" Aksel chuckled, his bushy gray eyebrows lifting, his leathery face wrinkling in a smile. "What are you worrying about? You'll be fowling soon enough. You might not find it so easy then. Look at me! A short stiff arm—that's what I got out of fowling." And he swung his injured right arm.

"And you got something else, too," Sven pointed

8

out. "Nobody's ever broken your record for most birds in a day, have they?"

"No, and nobody can give me back a useful right arm either," his uncle retorted. "There is a good reason for this rule of seventeen years before you go fowling. You are supposed to have got some sense in your head by then, and . . . psst!" He slapped at his chin, killing a long-legged insect which had alighted there. As he stared at it, his nephew was also slapping at another long-legged pest.

"Well, what do you make of that?" Aksel said, holding out the remains of the insect. "I haven't seen one for years. . ."

Sven looked at his uncle in amazement. "Why, there's thousands, millions of them on the island. It's only a *grindalokkur* (daddy longlegs). You must have seen them, Uncle."

Aksel Berge cocked an eyebrow. "If you'd let a man finish what he was saying, you'd understand what I was getting at," he pointed out. "Course I've seen *grindalokkur* on the island, but I haven't seen one down at *sea level* for years . . . maybe a dozen years." And rocking easily to the swaying of the boat he stood up and scanned the waters seaward.

When he sat down he shrugged, and almost at once was brushing at another of the long-legged *grindalokkur*. He struck another match, looked from under his bushy eyebrows at his nephew, then asked:

9

"Do you know what they reckon when *grindalokkur* are seen at sea level?"

"No. What?"

"They say that there are *grind* (caaing whales) in the neighborhood," Aksel commented. "That's why I looked south . . . but there's no sign of them yet."

"You're pulling my leg," Sven said. "There haven't been *grind* off Mykines for . . . well, I've never seen them, and I'm sixteen."

"That's a terrible old age, isn't it," his uncle chuckled. "You are right though—the *grind* have seemed to pass us by for long enough. It would be wonderful if we could get a *grindedrab* (whale-killing). Give us money for lots of things we need." He slapped again at another of the flies, and Sven waved a hand before his face as three more of the daddy longlegs fluttered over the boat.

Sven got to his feet, and with one foot on the gunwale to steady him against the pitching and rolling, shaded his eyes while he stared south. The sea was heaving, but with no whitecaps at all, which was most unusual. Between the lonely little island of Mykines and the coast line of Canada three thousand miles away there was nothing but sea. The long Atlantic rollers were seldom at rest, and this morning's quiet was ominous. Not that the sea was ever really quiet against the cliffs, which was why the small boat was pitching now.

As far as the eye could see there was deep, greenish blue, and not even the blob of a ship's hull to break the sky line. Freighters occasionally passed, bound from Scotland to Archangel in the White Sea, but they were few and far between. These seas were a lonely waste, where bad weather seemed to come to life in an hour.

Sven was about to drop back onto the seat when he saw a flicker of white. He stared, and a sudden excitement began to grow in him. That splash of foam was not natural.

Old Aksel sensed the sudden change in his nephew's attitude. "Well? Can you see something?"

"Wait—wait a minute!" Sven wanted to be sure. He had never before seen a school of the twelve- to twenty-foot-long caaing whales, the *grind* which set Faroe islanders half crazed with delight. He kept on staring, his eyes puckered against the sky glare.

The patch of foam was clearer now, and seemed to be drawing closer. There was white water filled with swimming black forms. It was incredible, but it looked as if the *grind* had at long last come to the waters of Mykines. In a voice half choked with excitement Sven turned and said, "Uncle, *grind!* Look, I'm sure I'm right. Hundreds of them. Hundreds!"

Old Aksel stood up, steadying himself against the rough wooden engine casing. He stared as Sven

11

had stared, only a little longer. He was trying to estimate the size of the school.

"Well?" Sven was almost dancing with impatience. "I'm right, aren't I?"

"Wrap your coat around an oar blade," Aksel ordered, turning around and staring up at the cliffs. "I don't know what the men are doing up there. They ought to have seen them long ago. *Grind! Grind!* GRIND!" He cupped his hands about his mouth and sent yell after yell up to the men fowling on the cliffs.

Sven was trembling with excitement as he tied his jacket around an oar blade. He knew well enough that this was the traditional way of signaling the approach of *grind*. A jacket on an oar blade could stop everything. No matter what work was going on, it would be dropped so that men and boys could rush for the boats. A school of caaing whales could bring more wealth than a month of good fishing.

"GRIND . . . GRIND . . . GRIND!" Sven waved his oar and joined his uncle in yelling the news, and it seemed to them both that the fowlers would never look down.

When they did, their reactions were immediate. The long-handled nets ceased to swing. The six men began to climb upward as if their lives depended on the speed with which they got to the cliff top.

Aksel turned to Sven, his face one huge grin.

"What a day, eh?" he chuckled. "I'll buy myself a new pipe out of this. We get the largest share for sighting the *grind*." He clapped his hands in glee and winked.

His smile vanished almost at once, however, when Sven scrambled over to him and started to crank the rickety little eight-horsepower engine.

"Here, wait a minute, Sven!" he protested. "We've still got the line out. What's the hurry?"

"Hurry! What about the *grind!*" Sven said impatiently. "If we don't get back to the landing they'll go without us. I'm not missing this, and—"

"You sit down, my lad!" his uncle ordered. "If you think we've had our line out all morning for nothing, you're mistaken!"

"But we can get fish any time!" Sven protested. "Look, I'll undo the line and tie it to—"

"You'll do nothing of the kind," Aksel said sternly. "There could be forty or fifty saithe waiting to be picked up. You remember this, Sven Klakk, an egg in the hand is better than a chicken on the wing any time. Because we've sighted *grind* doesn't mean that they'll be caught. They've got to be driven a good few miles before they can be cornered. That'll be somewhere around Vagar Island . . . there's no place on Mykines where the *grindedrab* can take place."

"You mean we're not going?" Sven's face was

13

pale, his mouth a thin line. He had listened many times to the older men talking of the excitement of a whale-killing, and the rejoicing which followed when the butchering was over and the meat and blubber had been divided up. Not to take part in the chase was like being told on your birthday that it was not your birthday after all.

"We are not going anywhere until we've got our line up," his uncle said. "You can start now if you like—and don't sulk. It isn't the end of the world."

Sven clambered back to the middle of the boat and began to haul in the long line. At any other time he would have been delighted with their catch, for almost every one of the plastic-covered hooks had a saithe on it.

"Now don't rush the job," his uncle cautioned. "It's better to coil the lines and hooks properly now, then they won't be in a tangle next time we come out."

Sven closed his eyes and bit back the angry words which tumbled to the tip of his tongue.

It seemed to him as if every fish he hauled aboard was determined to take up more time than usual. They fought madly, and seemed more slimy than ever before. By the time the last fish had been thrown on the heap, forty minutes had passed, and as Sven swung the starting handle of their engine his uncle said, "Oh-ho, here they come. My, it looks as if everybody's going out."

Sven turned and stared. The island's two largest motorized boats were each leading a string of half a dozen or so smaller boats. The engines were roaring at full throttle, and in the boats being towed men and boys were rowing to take some of the load. They were doing about six knots, and drew abreast rapidly.

"Uncle, let me go," Sven pleaded. "You could take the boat in alone, I know you could. You always were good at it."

Aksel did not say anything, but the expression on his face was sufficient. He knew, just as Sven knew, that a man needed two good arms to take a boat into the Mykines landing safely. To avoid disaster on the big slabs of rock which littered the approach to the landing, a man must have an expert eye, plus one hand on the tiller lines and another on the throttle.

"Look at them," Sven said miserably as the procession of boats stormed past. "They're even taking along young Hermann . . . and Olaf—he's only nine years old. Uncle!"

"Don't say 'Uncle' like that," Aksel said crossly. "Thank your lucky stars that we sighted the *grind*. At least we'll get a bigger share than anybody else. If they'd made the sighting from the cliff, we wouldn't have got anything."

"Look, we could both go," Sven said in final desperation. "We could—" And then he stopped.

There were times when Uncle Aksel could say more with a look than with words, and the look he gave Sven told the boy once and for all that they were *not* going.

Neither Sven nor Aksel spoke for the next ten minutes. Both stood swaying in their rocking, heaving boat, staring eastward as the two lines of boats grew smaller and smaller. The school of caaing whales must have moved fairly quickly along the coast, for when the boats finally disappeared from sight they were still going at their best speed, which meant the men had not yet sighted their quarry.

While Sven cranked the engine he was so preoccupied with his disappointment that he forgot a vital thing. Their rickety old engine was designed to use gasoline, but for economic running they always switched over to paraffin oil when the engine was really warmed up. They had been running on paraffin when they had shot their fishing line.

Sven did not switch over to gasoline, so each time he swung the starting handle he sucked more paraffin into the cylinders, and did not get even an apologetic cough from the engine. Finally Aksel, hiding a grin, said, "I usually try and start it on gasoline, Sven. It never was a good starter on paraffin."

"You knew all the time!" Sven shouted, his face flushed with anger.

"No . . . no, I didn't," Aksel protested. "No, I'd

16

have told you. It was only now that I saw the cock was turned the wrong way. Come on, lad, work your bad temper off on the oars. I know you think I've played a dirty trick on you, but what use would I have been if we had gone after the *grind*? Y'know, Sven, it isn't easy having only one good arm."

Sven stared at his uncle and was suddenly ashamed. He grinned sheepishly. "I'm sorry, Uncle," he said. "I am really—but I did want to go."

"There'll be another time," Aksel assured him. "Come on, now, let's get back. I could drink a whole pot of coffee."

There was no point in trying to start the engine now, for everything would be soaked in paraffin, so Sven got out the oars. As he pulled he began to feel better, and was back to his usual cheerful self by the time they got abreast of the village.

It was then they had the first inkling that something was wrong. From the cliffs—no more than sixty feet high at this point, Sven's grandfather, who was also Aksel's brother, appeared on the cliff top and began to make signs for them to turn back. He waved his arms and pointed toward the east.

"Keep rowing," Aksel ordered. "It isn't any use guessing what Napoleon wants."

By the time they drew near the landing there were a score of women waiting and, strangely enough, Arni, the assistant from the lighthouse on the smaller island of Mykinesholmur, was with them.

"Don't come in!" Grandfather Napoleon Berge shouted. "Start your engine and bring the boats back. It's urgent. Matter of life and death. Start your engine and bring the boats back!"

Startled, Sven and his uncle exchanged quick glances. Aksel shook his head. This was his boat, and he knew his engine. Having been soaked in paraffin, there was no hope of starting it for hours. The cylinders would have to dry out first.

"Row her in, Sven," he ordered. "We could never get this engine going."

3: The Gale Strikes

When it was obvious Sven was bringing the boat in, four of the younger women tucked their skirts above their knees and waded out to meet it. Even in the calmest weather landing was a tricky business. A boat had to come in riding a wave and then be hurriedly pulled out of reach of the backwash. No boats were ever left moored, for in the Faroes the weather can change in an hour, and this landing was exposed.

Usually there was laughter and joking as a boat was dragged in, but now there was a gloomy silence. When they had gotten it safely beyond the reach of the waves, Napoleon Berge called to his brother Aksel. "Couldn't you hear? We wanted you to bring the boats back at once. There's a—" He stopped then, for Aksel was shaking his head.

"We wouldn't have rowed back if we could have started the engine," he explained. "The cylinders are soaked in paraffin. What's wrong?"

19

There were muffled groans from the onlookers and two women turned away, biting their lower lips. Arni, a pale-faced Dane, came forward to explain about the S O S sent out by the *Faroes Seeker*.

"It will be hard enough for the crew," he pointed out, "for we have had a bad weather warning. A force ten gale is coming up from the northwest. If this injured man is not got ashore quickly, well . . ." He shrugged. There was no need for further explanations. A force ten gale around the Faroes usually meant two or three days of really bad weather.

Sven had listened with growing anxiety. His father was first mate on the schooner. He might even be the injured man. He turned to look at the boat, then at Aksel. His uncle, reading his thoughts, shook his head and murmured, "No, it's no use, Sven. It wouldn't start. I know my own engine too well."

"Well, isn't there something we can do?" Sven pleaded.

Grandfather Napoleon turned to him. "Sven, if you could get to the east end of the island you might be able to signal the boats. A smoke signal would bring them back in a hurry."

"Yes." Sven was glad to try anything. He rushed up the slope to their house, the farthest one from the landing. Hurriedly he pulled off his sea boots, and his mother, who had followed on his heels, handed him his sheepskin shoes as soon as he was ready for them.

Others had also been busy. One woman came with a bottle of paraffin. Another brought some slabs of peat. Old Napoleon Berge was ready with a box of matches. He was a tall man, and despite his years was still as erect as any guardsman. Tugging at his grizzled beard, he somehow managed a smile as he said, "This is your big chance, Sven. You always said you were a good runner. It's only four miles—if you can do it in twenty minutes you'll get the signal to them in time." He clapped his grandson encouragingly on the shoulder, but shook his head slowly as the boy started off.

There was no timekeeper to check when Sven finally got to the cliffs at the eastern end of Mykines. His time for the four miles was probably a record over such a course, for the island rose in tiers of ground that was pockmarked with puffin burrows, patches of quaking bog, and rock covered with no more than an inch of soil. It was hard going, particularly when the runner's feet were shod only in sheepskin shoes.

There was no sign of the boats in the stretch of water between Mykines and Vagar Island, but Sven did not despair. He broke his peat into small pieces, poured the paraffin over them, and struck a match. As flames rose he yanked up tufts of grass, and when the peat was beginning to glow he dropped the grass into the heart of the fire.

Not till then did he realize that there had been a change in the weather. The morning had been practically windless. Now, instead of rising in a straight column, the thick yellow smoke was whirled away, thinned out and dissipated before it had time to achieve "signal" strength.

Desperately Sven piled on more and more grass. He blew on the peat until it glowed pinky-white. The grass produced smoke, but the wind brushed it aside with ease.

Sven did not stop trying until the peat blocks had crumbled to a little pile of gray ash and the heat was no longer strong enough to burn the damp grass. Then he knew he had failed. Staring across to Vagar Island he saw dark shadows sweeping across the water, a sign of gusting winds. It was the beginning of the storm.

An hour later he arrived back in the village. There had been a considerable change at the landing since he and Uncle Aksel had come in. Waves were rolling in and beating themselves to foam, completely hiding the big slabs of rock. It was a familiar enough picture, and for the islanders held the same meaning as a closed door. Until the storm had beaten itself out, no one could land or put out from Mykines.

No one actually asked Sven if he had been successful. A young girl had been left to keep a lookout, and when she saw Sven coming she shouted the news. From the houses the women and the four old men left on Mykines emerged into the rising wind. Slowly they walked toward the Klakk house, and turned away sadly as soon as Sven shook his head.

His mother, Maria, poured a mug of coffee, then brought out another pair of dry sheepskin shoes. Sven looked at her, wondering what she had in mind.

"At the lighthouse they'll want to know what happened," she said.

"Well, isn't there anybody—" Sven began, then stopped. For the first time it struck him that there wasn't anybody else. He remembered being upset that even boys as young as Hermann and Olaf had gone with the boats. Out of the whole population of some hundred and fifty people there were only four men left behind—two who were very old, plus Grandfather and Uncle Aksel; and boys under the age of eight. The rest were women and girls.

By now the first real gusts were beginning to whistle and screech over the village. Many of the houses had turf roofs, and all of them were held down to bedrock by stanchions. When the northern Atlantic was in an angry mood no house would have remained standing if it hadn't been fastened down to the rock by strong cables.

As Sven left for his mile and a half trip to the lighthouse on Mykinesholmur he had to bend to the wind. Odd flurries of rain drove almost horizontally and stung like tiny pellets. The landing was now just an angry welter of foam, the breaking waves already reaching thirty feet above where Sven and his uncle had landed such a short time earlier.

The tiny island of Mykinesholmur was separated from Mykines itself by a deep chasm. It was as if some giant had sliced off the smaller island with a mighty axe stroke. Across this chasm a narrow strip of steel bridge acted as a connection.

Even in calm weather there was always noise and confusion below the bridge, for waves from the northwest roared in to meet waves coming in from the southeast. They met like knights at a joust, crashing to foam and flinging spray, pebbles, and even rocks as high as the bridge itself. Twice in the past the bridge had been smashed by rocks; but now the narrow ribbon was of steel and was usually only dented and rusted when the winter storms were over.

Sven had to run the gauntlet of clouds of spray, and he hunched down with his head tucked deep into his collar as he struggled across. The wind was much stronger here, as if the gap between the two islands were an escape hatch for the storm's wrath. The handrails quivered and thrummed in sympathy with the titanic battle going on below.

By the time he had climbed the three hundred feet to the lighthouse, Sven was reeling. The wind was like a demon, plucking and buffeting him, making his eyes stream tears, and at times taking his breath.

Arni must have been watching, for he came to the door and hauled the battered youngster inside. The door was slammed and a wooden bar swung across it. The lighthouse was as strongly built as man could devise, yet it quivered almost continuously under the wind blasts.

The wife of the lighthouse keeper brought Sven a cup of coffee and took his spray-soaked coat. Then as she took off his dripping shoes she looked up, a quick, almost shy smile on her face. "My husband has got contact with the schooner, Sven," she said. "They could not do it from Thorshavn, but Edvin has managed it. I think everything will be all right. Go up when you have drunk the coffee. He will give you the news."

Sven gulped down his coffee and was directed up to the radio-room. This was the first time he had been inside the lighthouse, but he had no curiosity about the various rooms. All he wanted was to hear from Edvin Christiansen the latest news.

There was not much to tell. Somehow, perhaps because the lighthouse was so much higher than the radio station at Thorshavn, Christiansen had been able to pick out from the background hum the vague mutter of Morse. He had spoken to the *Faroes Seeker* and was being received quite well. The schooner, battened down against the storm, was in no immediate danger. Every possible precaution was being taken. A jury rudder had been fixed, and a sea anchor, as strong and heavy as possible, had been put over the bows. As a result the schooner was bows on to the rising seas, and drifting with the wind.

Mrs. Christiansen thought Sven should stay a little longer at the lighthouse, but he insisted he must get back to give the news to the anxious people on Mykines.

He went down the slope, the wind tearing at him like an angry demon, and it was only when he reached the bridge that he hesitated. In the hour between his first crossing and now the situation had grown much worse. The thunder of breaking seas in the channel between the two islands was infinitely greater and the spray was obscuring the bridge completely. When Sven edged nearer and laid a hand on the rail, he could feel the impulses going through the whole structure as big stones thrown up from below struck the bridge.

He turned back, but after going some twenty yards he stopped and looked again at the bridge. If he delayed his return, his mother would worry. She might even think he had been swept off the bridge. And the rest of the women who had husbands or sons on the *Faroes Seeker*—they would want the news. The word was not so wonderful, but it was better than thinking the schooner had sunk.

Reluctantly Sven ventured once more onto the quaking, trembling bridge. Below him the chasm seemed filled with a roaring, yeasty froth. He had never seen it so bad, and the screaming wind jammed him against the right-hand rail, jarring his ribs.

Had it been night he might have gone on and been killed. As it was, he moved a few more feet nearer the center of the bridge, and then, as if giving him a last warning, a huge piece of rounded rock hurtled up amid a shower of smaller stones. It was lost for a second in the steamy mist of spray, then fell back onto the bridge with a crash which made the metalwork shiver in every bolt and rivet.

Sven was forced to retreat. He slept the night in the lighthouse. Twice during the next day he went down to the bridge, and had to turn back; but the second time he saw his mother on the far side. It was impossible to get any message to her by word of mouth, but he did give her the "thumbs-up" sign. She understood and motioned to him to go back to the lighthouse.

During his second day with the Christiansens and Arni they got the news from Thorshavn that the Norwegian rescue ship had been forced to turn back. With fuel running low, and two seamen injured from being thrown off their feet, the vessel was putting back to the Shetland port of Lerwick. If the weather abated she would return again in about forty-eight hours.

It was becoming increasingly difficult to pick out the Morse signal from the *Faroes Seeker*. The schooner's radio was running on batteries since the engines had been put out of action, and the power was failing.

They had been informed that the injured man was no worse, though in great pain. The vessel, helpless before the storm, was now taking some water, but the crew were manning the pumps and keeping the water under control.

Then, just as darkness came, they lost contact.

Edvin Christiansen, proud of his skill with the radio, tried every trick he knew in an effort to conjure out of the ether a flicker of dots and dashes which would tell him the *Faroes Seeker* was still alive and on the air. When he finally took off the headset he was haggard-faced.

"Go to bed, Sven," he said gently. "If you can sleep, it will be better. At least one cannot worry when one is asleep. Arni, I must have a few hours' rest. Call me if you get any sign from them."

When his wife asked him what was happening he slowly shook his head. The glass was beginning to rise, but he had a feeling that the better weather was coming too late.

Sven brought his improvised bed into the watch-room and Arni was glad of some company. They connected the alarm bell which rang automatically if any message came through on the radio, and tuned again to the wave length the schooner had been using before.

Having done all they could, Sven and Arni tried to sleep, but the storm kept them awake. The lighthouse was still trembling under the buffeting of the wind. Its high-pitched wails as it beat against the walls sometimes sounded like the screams of a terrified child. As a background to the wind, the thunder of waves breaking against the foot of the cliffs went on continuously—grumble-crash, grumble-crash, never varying, going on as if it would never end.

Arni lay listening, occasionally opening an eye and looking toward the radio. He was almost willing the alarm bell to ring and tell him someone was sending a message; but the sound never came. At last he drifted off to sleep. Sleep had already claimed Sven. Rain battered the windows but neither of them heard it.

The only thing which seemed alive was the metal finger on the barograph which recorded on a slowly turning drum the pressure outside. Just before the storm began, the finger had traced a steep fall; now it was inking in an equally steep rise. The bad weather was ending.

In the light-room the brilliant beam flashed its course through the night, showing the rain stabbing down like a million little spears, each a glistening silver.

An hour before dawn Arni suddenly opened his eyes. He had slouched in the easy chair, and he lifted a hand to rub his stiff neck. Then, as he realized where he was and that he was on duty, apprehension filled his eyes. He turned to look at the clock, then glanced guiltily down at Sven, who was still sleeping.

Quickly Arni filled in his night log, showing "Nothing to report" at one o'clock, three o'clock, five o'clock. This done, he went up to the light-room to make sure all was well there.

A minute later he tumbled back down the ladder. After giving Sven a hard shake, he grabbed a hand-signaling lamp and turned back toward the light-chamber. Sven rolled over in bed as Arni hurried from the room, and something about the urgency of his movements swept sleep from the youngster's eyes at once.

Wiping his mouth with the back of his hand he went to the foot of the ladder leading to the lamp-chamber and called up, "Is something the matter?"

"Call Mr. Christiansen!" Arni shouted back.

"There's a light out there! Somebody is signaling to us—it might be the schooner!"

When Edvin Christiansen, a bathrobe slung over his shoulders, got to the lamp-room there was an air of joy about the place. Sven and Arni were both pressing noses against the thick glass, and out in the darkness a tiny point of light was appearing and disappearing; sometimes it was no more than a flicker, then it would show for a longer time. It was Morse, dots and dashes from a vessel which appeared to be about half a mile from the rocky coast line.

"It *is* the schooner, Mr. Christiansen"—Arni could not keep the excitement from his voice—"and the injured man is still alive. They are asking if we can do anything. The crew are exhausted; they have been pumping continuously for two days and nights. They had no power. What shall I say?"

Edvin Christiansen stared out into the darkness. The flickering light was not showing now. The signaler on the *Faroes Seeker* had given his news and asked his question. Now he was waiting for an answer.

Sven had stepped back from the window and was looking anxiously at Christiansen. Deep down he knew there was no answer. He had lived by and on the sea all his life. He knew ships, he knew Mykines and the cliffs. What could one do for a helpless ship? Nothing!

"Tell him"—Christiansen paused while he passed his tongue across his upper lip—"tell him we are waking the islanders. If there is anything we can do—we'll do it." He was shaking his head as he finished, but catching Sven's anxious stare he said quickly, "Don't worry, boy. The battle is never lost until it is over. And it does sound as if the wind is dropping."

He turned and went down to the room below. When Sven joined him he was studying the barograph. "See that—the glass is rising," he said with a smile. "The storm will have blown itself out in an hour or so. It is always so when the glass rises so quickly.

"Now let's go downstairs and I'll make some coffee. Then you must try and get across the bridge. Waken everybody on Mykines. Tell them I'm going to signal the schooner and ask them to try and fire a line ashore if they get close enough. If they can do that, we might save them yet."

Arni had come in as the lighthouse keeper was finishing. He gave Christiansen a startled glance, then opened his mouth as if he were about to protest. Whatever he was going to say died on his lips as the lighthouse keeper led Sven toward the door, at the same moment lifting a quick finger to his assistant in a signal for silence.

Telling Sven to start the oil stove in the kitchen and put water on for coffee, Christiansen turned to

Arni when they were alone, and with a sad shake of his head murmured, "I know what you were going to say, Arni—I could see it in your face."

"But why fool the boy into thinking there is a chance, Mr. Christiansen?" Arni protested. "You are giving him hope when, unless a miracle happens, there is no hope."

"I know all that," Christiansen agreed, giving Arni a resigned shrug. "But why kill hope in the boy right away? Miracles have happened before today. Let him go down and tell the islanders. It will give him a little time to get used to the idea that the schooner is going to be wrecked. God help the crew, for I know we can't."

The two men stood for a few moments in silence, then Arni walked toward the door.

"I'll signal them to try and fire a rocket line ashore," he said, "but this is going to be a sad day for the people of Mykines. About half the crew come from the island, don't they?"

Christiansen nodded. Only when he joined Sven in the kitchen did he manage to conjure up an encouraging smile. That smile was a silent lie, for he knew there was practically no hope for the *Faroes Seeker*. She was a doomed ship.

4: A Lone Swimmer
Gets Ashore

While Sven was watching the water coming to a boil for coffee, Edvin Christiansen wakened his wife. He gave her the news about the helpless schooner.

"Go in and make sure the boy eats a good breakfast," he urged. "He will want to get over to his people as quickly as possible, but it is better that he has a full belly before he goes. There is the bridge to cross, and he is sure to get a soaking."

He went out to test the storm and came back looking pleased. The viciousness was going out of the wind. Instead of a continuous screaming fury, it was now gusting, as if it had grown tired of battering the two islands without success.

Mrs. Christiansen prepared a good meal and refused to listen to Sven's pleas that he did not have time to eat. "It is still dark outside," was her calm retort, "and every minute the storm grows quieter.

Remember, Sven, you have the bridge to cross, and a half-hour's delay is better than being blown off it."

They saw him on his way as adequately clothed against the storm as possible, but even the sou'wester and oilskins could not keep him dry when he reached the bridge. There was no longer the devil's tattoo of pebbles and stones beating on the underside of the steel bridge walk, but high-flung spray and even great soapsud patches of spume filled the air. By the time he was across and back on Mykines, water was running down his neck.

He hardly felt the discomfort of it, however, for once the bridge was behind, new hope surged within him. For nearly three days he had been cut off from his mother. Now he had good news. The schooner was afloat, the storm was dying down, and he refused to believe the little voice at the back of his mind which kept reminding him of the towering cliffs, the awesome rocks, and the current which would surely take the schooner inshore.

Each house on Mykines stood by itself, and Sven's was at the eastern end of the village. No light showed anywhere, but a few moments after his first knock on the door his mother let him in.

Maria Klakk must have been sleeping with one eye open, since she had everything ready for an emergency. The fire in the big stove showed that, for it was easily brought to a fierce heat by a minute of blowing with the sheepskin bellows.

Napoleon Berge listened to his grandson's story, and took command at once.

"Waken everybody," he ordered. "Tell your Uncle Aksel he must bring all the rope he has. Tell the women, too, to bring ropes. Maria, you had better organize the older women. They must make plenty of good coffee and soup. When we get the men ashore they'll need something to put life into them again."

The little voice of reason at the back of Sven's mind, which had kept telling him rescue was impossible, suddenly lost its power to frighten the boy. Grandfather seemed so sure they could save the schooner's crew; there was not a shadow of doubt in his voice.

The moment the door closed on Sven, however, Maria Klakk looked at her father and her face was somber.

"You don't believe we can get them ashore—not in this wind."

"I'm not believing anything, Maria," her father said soberly, "but the man who is ready . . . well, he can always take advantage of a miracle."

Maria Klakk swallowed the lump in her throat. Napoleon Berge had always been like that: stubborn, refusing to face facts. As if reading her thoughts, the old man came across the room and laid an arm around her shoulders.

"Maria, if it is God's will, they will live," he said gently. "But we must be ready to help."

When Sven came back, lights were showing in most houses, and if anything his hopes were even higher than before. In the past half-hour the wind had dropped considerably. The storm was rapidly blowing itself out.

In the cold gray of early morning a score of women, along with Sven, his Uncle Aksel, and his grandfather, stood just beyond reach of the waves thundering up the slipway. Somewhere out in the murk and the breaking seas was the *Faroes Seeker*. They should see her soon, for already there were gaps in the fiercely scudding blanket of dark gray clouds.

There was a constant, high-pitched chattering from the slipway as each wave threw up tons of coarse gravel, then dragged it back in the powerful undertow. Above that grinding of stone a woman's voice rose in a scream, and she pointed excitedly out to sea.

Within thirty seconds everyone had sighted the schooner. The vessel was driving slowly eastward. She had lost one mast, and there was a remnant of sail flapping from her mainmast. The crew had not just waited for disaster, but had tried to keep some way on their ship.

The *Faroes Seeker* was riding with her bows into the wind, kept thus by a massive sea anchor paid out from her foredeck. She drifted along immersed in a continuous patch of foam. Now that she had come abreast of Mykines the rocky coast line was throwing back the surge of the Atlantic rollers, and as a result the seas were more broken. The vessel was taking a worse hammering now than at any time during the storm. She pitched and reeled like a drunken man.

No one spoke as the schooner drifted closer. She was little more than a hundred and fifty yards from the coast, and appeared to be moving even closer in. Women with sons or husbands aboard were praying that she might come close enough for a line to be got ashore.

There was no sign of life on her until she was abreast of the landing, then a light flickered in the wheelhouse. A few moments later a man could be seen at the wheelhouse window.

"Are you ready, Sven?" Napoleon Berge asked. "He's going to fire a rocket."

Sven inched out of the little crowd. He had a rope tied about his waist. There was an old cork life jacket fastened about his chest—a life jacket washed ashore years ago. In addition he was wearing two pairs of thick trousers and his hips were padded with sacks.

If the line came inshore he was to dash down and try to retrieve it. No one had any illusions about the dangers of such a move. The waves sweeping up the slipway could pick up a man and grind the life out of him in a matter of minutes if he should be thrown off his feet.

The extra clothing and the cork life belt were to take the first savage blows if the sea did get its cruel claws into Sven. The stout line about his waist would make sure he was not dragged out to sea.

From the schooner came a sudden stab of flame, and everyone watching held his breath as the rocket soared into the air. The man with the rocket gun had waited for the right moment. He wanted to fire when the wind had dropped, and for a second or so success seemed certain.

The tiny pencil of flame showing at the back of the rocket indicated that it was bringing the life line right across to the landing. Sven inched forward, muscles taut, his eyes on the waves. He must dash down while the undertow of a wave was racing back to the sea. To run down when a wave was coming up would have been madness.

A chorus of shouts from the crowd made him lift his eyes for an instant, and he groaned when he saw what was happening. At the vital moment when the rocket was at its highest point a sudden fierce gust of wind swept it off course as if it were no more than a feather.

The spurting flame drifted eastward, and the rocket plunged into the sea some twenty yards east of the landing. For the next few minutes there was frenzied activity aboard the schooner as men hauled in the dripping line, with the idea of firing a second rocket; but the chance had gone. The wind and the current took the vessel steadily away from the landing, the one point where a line might have been got ashore.

Without a word Sven untied the line from his waist, and his mother took off his life belt. While the little crowd moved away from the landing and began to walk eastward, following the schooner, Sven rid himself of his protective sacking and the extra pair of trousers.

Carrying their ropes, though there seemed no possible chance of them being used now, the women walked slowly along the edge of the cliffs, keeping pace with the drifting *Faroes Seeker*.

There were no tears. For centuries this tiny island had had to fight its own battles. Even now, though they had the radio telephone in the Mykinesholmur lighthouse, they could still be cut off for weeks. There was no possible place for a landing field for even the tiniest aircraft, and the heavy mists that frequently veiled the island made even helicopter landings unpredictable.

When they had gone some two miles along the cliffs, and the land was beginning to slope down from six hundred feet to a mere two hundred and fifty feet, a breathless Arni joined them.

He brought news that in response to Edvin Christiansen's plea one of the Faroes' interisland boats had left Thorshavn in a desperate attempt to reach the schooner before she went ashore.

"Well, aren't you glad?" Arni asked when neither Napoleon nor Aksel Berge showed much enthusiasm. Sven watched his grandfather and his uncle anxiously. They knew, better than anyone else, what hope there was for the men on the schooner.

Aksel Berge shrugged and looked at Napoleon. The older man shook his head slowly as he explained, "Even in calm weather it takes an interisland boat two hours to get here, Arni. Two hours! She won't be afloat two hours from now." And he pointed a long finger down toward the schooner.

"It won't be two hours from now!" Arni snapped. "Mr. Christiansen called Thorshavn as soon as young Sven left the lighthouse, and the boat left within minutes."

"Well, I suppose they might—" There Napoleon stopped, interrupted by a shriek of horror from one of the women.

All eyes were turned again toward the white-splashed sea. During the past ten minutes the *Faroes Seeker* had been taking a worse battering than ever. The coast at this point had a long, sickle-shaped indentation, and the seas were rougher in the shallow bay.

The sea anchor was still keeping the vessel's bows pointing toward the waves, but her afterdeck seemed more under water than above. A few moments before the warning scream the schooner had taken a sea aboard on her for'ard quarter, and the tons of foam-flecked water had made her reel.

Like a tired swimmer she had struggled upward, but for seconds her afterdeck had been hidden under a roaring flood. Then, in a sudden flurry of foam, something went over the starboard stern rail. From the cliff top it looked as if someone had upset a box of giant matches . . . and in the middle of them was a swimmer!

If the men in the schooner's wheelhouse saw the man they made no attempt to throw either a life belt or a rope. Perhaps they were unable to see him. The ship staggered on while the tiny form in the foam swam about amid the clutter of broken planking—for the things which looked from the cliff like matches were broken timbering, planks and struts.

There were only ten women on the cliff top—each of whom had either a husband or a son among the schooner's crew. Napoleon Berge had ordered the others back to the houses, to look after the children and to make soups, coffee, and prepare beds just in case there were survivors.

For perhaps three minutes even the women kept silent. Like Sven, Napoleon, Aksel, and the two leathery-faced eighty-year-olds who had insisted on coming, they were waiting for that tiny figure to disappear. They knew these seas; the awful power of the waves. One woman broke the silence with a cry when a wave surged by, lifting both planks and swimmer. It dropped them down into the trough, all tumbling together like beans shaken into the bottom of a handkerchief.

Sven Klakk was not the only one whose eyes shut instinctively. As a much younger boy he had once fallen overboard along with some light timbering, and had been unmercifully bruised in seas very much calmer than these.

Yet when he did look again the swimmer was still there—not among the planks and pieces of timber, but a littler nearer the cliffs. He was swimming toward the shore! Eight of the ten women announced the fact at the same moment and looked toward Napoleon, waiting for him to say what could be done. He shook his head. There was a time for optimism, and a time when you had to face hard facts.

"It is no use hoping!" he shouted. "I think we should get down on our knees and pray. Only God can help him now. No man could swim ashore—no man!"

Sven plucked at Napoleon's arm, and his blue eyes were alive with new hope as he shouted: "Grandfather—the Inlet. He's making for the Inlet. If he can get through he'll be safe. The waves never break badly in there."

For a moment Napoleon Berge hesitated. Then he nodded to Sven. "Yes, if he could get through to the Inlet he would be all right. Come on."

The Inlet was a tiny fjord which ran some eighty yards into the face of the cliff. Its entrance at the sea edge was no more than thirty feet wide, and for forty yards the waves boomed through a corridor of the same width. Then the fjord suddenly widened to more than three times that width, and as a result waves which were like rampaging monsters at the fjord entrance were immediately robbed of their power. A twenty-foot wave would be flattened in a second to one of six feet.

Countless centuries earlier the Inlet had begun where a small stream ran over the edge of the cliff. Gradually it had cut a path through the rock, and even more gradually the fjord had been born. The little stream was still cutting a path through the rock, but now its course was eighty yards in from the sea, and the water trickled down a gully which everyone on Mykines knew as the Chimney.

Generations of Mykines children had dared one

another to go down the Chimney during the short summer months. There was not a parent on the island who hadn't warned his sons and daughters not to go down that slippery rock cutting; and there was not a child worth his salt who hadn't gone down anyway into the eerie half-light of the Inlet.

It was not a particularly dangerous climb down the Chimney, for the water had worn a tortuous course through the softer parts of the rock, wriggling here and there, sometimes widening out, sometimes following a narrow track, and ending finally on a great bank of sand and stones at the landward end of the fjord.

Napoleon led the way to the brink of the Inlet. At cliff top height it was a kind of Huntsman's Leap, less than twenty feet across in places, and there was always a hollow booming noise coming up from the passage below through which the sea washed even at low tide.

The pale form of the swimmer was still some seventy yards or so from the Inlet entrance. The great waves lifted him up, then dropped him down the back into the trough as if he were no more than a piece of flotsam. He was making progress, but only slowly.

"He'll never have the strength to swim in," one woman said, and Sven's mother turned on her like a tigress. "He has come half the distance, hasn't he?" she said angrily. "Why shouldn't he do it? He *will* do it. Father, what can we do to help him?"

"Well, somebody's got to get down into the Inlet—by the Chimney," Napoleon said gravely. "There has always been a strong undertow down there, and I doubt if he'd have the strength to climb out onto the bank by himself. Sven, you'd better go down. Take a rope, and when you get to the bottom fasten one end to something, and the other around your waist. If he gets so far he won't have much strength left, and—"

"Is there time?" Sven asked.

"There won't be time if you stand there talking," Napoleon said. "Grab a rope and get across to the Chimney. You can be down in a quarter of an hour." And he turned to the nearest woman, holding out his hands for her rope.

"Grandfather, it isn't any use going down the Chimney," Sven said defiantly. "Look—he's nearer now. He'll be in the gap within ten minutes."

They all looked down again, and despite the great waves which lifted the swimmer and then seemed to suck him seaward, he was nearer the towering rock walls and the thirty-foot gap.

There was despair in the eyes of most of the women. None of them knew who the swimmer was. He might be the husband or son of one of them, and they were gripped by the numb fears which

46

come when someone is in danger and not a hand can be lifted to help.

It was Sven who electrified them all. An idea had come to him—an idea which sent a shiver of apprehension through him. But it seemed the only way to get help to the struggler below.

"I'll—I could go over the cliff. I could get in that way—quickly."

"No—no, it's too dangerous!" Maria Klakk protested immediately, the color draining from her face.

"It might be Sven's father," Napoleon said soberly. For a second or so the old man and his daughter stared into each other's eyes, then Maria Klakk nodded.

In a second the little group woke to frenzied life. Each woman carried a long length of fowling rope. With skill born of long practice the ropes were laid out and knotted together. Aksel Berge fastened the rope about Sven's waist, then superintended his slide over the cliff edge.

There was no question of being lowered into the Inlet itself, for the rock face bulged in such a manner that no climber, even with the aid of a rope, could have clung to the rock.

Six women paid out the rope. Two others made sure that there were no kinks in it. Aksel Berge lay flat on the cliff top to watch Sven's descent. Napoleon stood and watched, his face betraying none of the fears which were making his heart beat so fast. But the fingers of his right hand "combed" his beard, always a sign that he was worried.

Like most Mykines men he had been a fowler, and he knew the dangers of cliff work. The first essential of a good fowler was caution, and steadiness in descent. If Sven was to be on hand when the lone swimmer got into the Inlet he must go down very quickly, and the women were seeing that he did just that.

Sven's heart was hammering against his ribs for the first half-minute of his descent. Then he was too busy to be frightened. Not only did it need swift hand work and footwork to keep clear of the innumerable ledges, but he had the problem of startled and angry sea birds to contend with.

Guillemots and a few skuas rose with startled, angry squawks as he slid over the ledges on which they were resting. Some planed down toward the sea, glad to get away from the danger. Others began to mob Sven. They wheeled about him, wings flapping within inches of his head and shoulders, and filled the air with their raucous screams and squawks. There was barely a moment when a yellow beak or orange legs didn't slither within a foot of Sven's head.

Sometimes he struck a ledge with a foot, and as his downward descent was slowed for a moment the rope slackened. When he slid off the ledge again, it was with a jerk which tightened the rope about his chest and made him gasp.

At seventy feet from the sea he was already being wet by upflung spray. This was the danger point. He had to stop here, then work his way around the corner into the Inlet. If he went much lower, the rocks would be too slippery with spray for him to keep a grip.

He grabbed at a ledge when he was sixty feet from the sea, and four very surprised guillemots went streaking off the ledge as if a bomb had exploded among them. Sven gave a hurried jerk on the rope, signal for those above to stop lowering. Then he looked around for his next move.

He would have to move into the jaws of the Inlet now, keeping at the same height until he was all the way inside, for the waves charging in from the Atlantic were passing right beneath him.

For the next four minutes he worked with a skill which would have brought nods of satisfaction from the most expert fowler. He kept signaling for more rope, and finally reached the place where the Inlet suddenly widened out into a huge roofless cavern.

He paused for a moment, looked down, and noted with growing hope that the mighty waves pulsing in through the thirty-foot gap were losing their force as soon as they came to the wide part. But from his height he could see the vicious undertow at work. The waves, though reduced to some five feet in height, charged up the steep sloping bank of gravel and sand, barely reached the far rock wall, and then slithered back, taking with them tons of stones which roared and chattered in an ear-tingling discord of crashing water and grinding rock.

Seeing the thrust and backsweep of the waves spurred Sven on. If the lone swimmer did get here he would probably be far too exhausted to battle with such a powerful undertow. He must have help the moment he got into the shallower water.

Sven took risks getting down which would have made his mother close her eyes in fear and dread if she had been able to see him. But his sheepskin-clad feet never slipped, and when he was only about six feet from the top of the sand and gravel slope, he pulled more rope in—then jumped.

Waves were curling to within a foot or so of him, but they were not getting all the way back to the rock wall itself.

It was hard work now to drag spare rope in, but Sven hauled more along and sought a place where he could snub his line. He wanted to leave himself with twenty or thirty feet to spare, so that if need be he could rush into the water and grab the swimmer.

Sven was like a runner now, waiting for the race to begin; but still there was no sign of the laboring seaman ploughing his way through the waves. Minute after minute passed, and Sven's hopes dwindled. He began to be haunted by a fear that, with strength failing, the man from the *Faroes Seeker* had perhaps been dashed against the rock walls of the Inlet.

Then, quite suddenly, the swimmer arrived. He must have been half submerged by the wave which bore him in. The five-foot wall of water broke half way up the stony bank. Its foam licked up and up, to within a yard of where Sven stood. Then, defeated, the water went back, taking gravel with it and filling the air again with the grinding chatter.

In that moment Sven saw the swimmer. He was on all fours, with water and stones slithering past him. It was the moment Sven had waited for. This was the time for a quick rush forward. He had already planned what he would do. He would slip his rope about the man's waist, locking them both together, then they would begin the climb up the bank to a spot where the next wave could not reach them.

It was all clear in Sven's mind—but he did not move. The swimmer was not his father. He was not even a member of the schooner's crew. This valiant swimmer who had defeated the great Atlantic rollers was not even a man, but an animal—a most unexpected animal. It was a big, cream-colored polar bear!

5: Trapped!

Weeks earlier the polar bear had made a kill of a big seal on the fringe of ice up the Davis Straits. He had gorged until his hunger was satisfied and then had gone to sleep near the remains of his prize. When he awoke he ate more of the meat, and only then did he discover that he was a long way from the coast of Greenland where he had spent the whole of his five years of life.

There was only a vague suggestion of land far to the east. The ice on which he had made his kill was no more than a small berg which had been grounded for a few hours. It had refloated while the bear slept, and carried away from the shore by the southern current, was now on its way toward the Atlantic Ocean.

In the full power of his summer strength the bear walked endless miles round and round the ice as it drifted farther away from land, and ever nearer the warmer zone where it would eventually melt away completely.

Each day the iceberg grew smaller, and each day the bear lost some of his full-fed sleekness. Several times he plunged into the sea with the intention of swimming to land. Each time instinct told him that land was too far distant and he returned to the berg.

From being sleek and well padded his body shrank until his skin hung in folds along his flanks. Finally, too weak even to stand, he flopped down on the ice. Death from starvation was no more than a few days distant.

It was then that the *Faroes Seeker* came along. She was heading south, her holds full of prime cod, gutted, flaked, and salted, all ready for the final processing in Thorshavn before being dispatched to markets in Germany, Spain, and South America.

By this time the berg was no more than a large ice pan, and someone on the schooner, chancing to turn his binoculars on the ice, saw the bear. The master of the *Faroes Seeker* was called. Since he had once before bought a bear skin and sold it in Copenhagen for five hundred kroner, he hove to and sent the longboat across. A halt of half an hour for a 500-kroner prize was well worth it.

For some minutes after the men landed on the ice floe it was touch and go whether the bear would be butchered on the spot and skinned at once. Then someone suggested that a live polar bear might be worth many times the price of a skin. European zoos were always on the lookout for good specimens.

The half-hour halt developed into a two-hour struggle to get the limp beast aboard. A stout wooden pen was built in the stern, and three men agreed to take turns in nursing the animal back to life. Tinned milk for two days did the trick, and the crew agreed to sacrifice their small supply of frozen mutton in order to keep the bear's strength up.

There was a general air of excitement aboard the schooner. According to the master a good live specimen polar bear could bring as much as sixteen thousand kroner, and he agreed that the money would be shared equally by everyone. It was an unexpected bonus which, on top of a good season with the cod, put the crew in high spirits.

Within a week the bear was padding backward and forward in the confined space of his wooden cage, and eating everything put in for him. He began to look much better. Then, with the end of the trip almost in sight, came the collision which culminated in the engine room explosion, followed by the force ten gale. From then on the bear had neither food nor drink.

His cage had been well made, but its position on the afterdeck exposed it to every wave which crashed aboard. Gradually the bolt holes in the wooden struts weakened, and the whole structure was in a precarious state when the schooner began to drift past Mykines Island in the first gray of dawn.

As it drew near the Inlet an extra large wave crashed aboard. With the lurching of the schooner the weakened bolt holes broke and in seconds the cage disintegrated. The whole structure was swept over the side, taking the prisoner with it.

Most animals would not have survived, but the polar bear is almost as much at home in water as it is on land. When the cage hit the water and broke up completely the bear struck out, swimming anywhere for the first minute in an effort to gain his freedom.

Then, as the *Faroes Seeker* drifted eastward, the bear saw the loom of the cliffs. They promised safety and perhaps the food he craved. Not until he was within a hundred yards of the rocky walls did he see the black slit which was the opening into the Inlet. Calling on his reserves of strength, he survived wave after wave until he was swept into the channel leading into the Inlet itself.

Now, standing inches deep in gravel and sand, the bear faced Sven Klakk. His flanks were heaving mightily as he fought for breath; his legs were shaking from the struggle of the past few minutes. For the moment he had done all he could do, and must rest.

Sven, for his part, just stood and stared, petrified with astonishment. He recognized the animal.

Mykines was isolated, but for many years had had its little school and its quota of books. In one of them Sven had seen pictures of polar bears, and the men who went year after year to the Davis Straits after cod often spoke of the mighty, cream-colored beasts which haunted the shores of Greenland.

What Sven never expected was to come face to face with a polar bear at a moment when he had been keyed up to rescue a half-drowned seaman. For perhaps fifteen seconds animal and boy faced each other, and then the next wave broke in a hissing thunder on the stony sandbank.

It curled up the bear's flanks, and as the undertow rushed back again the bear moved. His great weight, almost a thousand pounds, was beginning to sink his four paws deeper and deeper into the sand. The gravel started to slide backward toward the sea, taking him with it.

With a ponderous lunge the bear began to climb up the bank, almost falling on his nose as he struggled to drag his forepaws out of the sand. For a moment or so it seemed as if he might be defeated and overwhelmed by the next wave; but he was a fighter, and somehow pulled himself free and shuffled upward.

The paralysis which had chained Sven to the spot was broken. With a yell of fear he turned, and rushing to his right, made a mighty leap for a ledge a few feet up the rocky wall.

Fear added spring to his muscles, and like a cat going up a garden wall he heaved himself a clear ten feet from the sand. Only when he tried to haul himself even higher did he realize that he had chosen a bad spot. The rock face above him was without niche or cranny for almost a yard. He looked about in desperation, but there was no way he could climb. To get out of the Inlet now he would have to drop back to the sand, then start his climb from a yard or so to the left.

His rope couldn't give him any help. He had snubbed it around a finger of rock just above the high-water mark, and the rope trailed loosely down the rock face, across the sand. If the bear found the rope and looped a paw through it, Sven could be plucked off his ledge with one quick heave.

For the next five minutes, however, nothing happened. Waves crashed in continually, but the bear was content to slump out of their reach while some of his spent strength returned. Sven's anxiety grew. He was standing on a very narrow ledge, his weight more or less on his toes, and already he could feel the strain on his calf muscles. It would not be long before cramp attacked him.

Then the bear got to his feet. He was desperately hungry, and in his eyes anything which moved spelled food. He came to the foot of the rock face below Sven, looked up and whined.

Sven stared down, and his wildly beating heart

contracted even more with fear as he realized how emaciated the animal was. He couldn't see the bear's ribs—his thick, water-laden fur hid them. But the way the fur hung in folds told its own story of near starvation.

For perhaps thirty seconds nothing happened, then the bear heaved himself to an upright position, steadied himself with his left paw and swung his right in an effort to sweep Sven off his perch. Only then was it possible to see what a magnificent creature he had been. His weight was so great that his hind feet began to dig into the wet sand, and water formed tiny pools about them.

It was the very softness of the wet sand which defeated the bear. He lunged upward, and the wet sand gave so that his rear feet dug down several inches; just enough to keep the thick, immensely strong claws from catching Sven's feet.

After several attempts the bear retreated and squatted on his haunches like a man pondering a problem. Then he came back and made a determined effort to climb the rock face. But even his hair-coated paws could not get a grip on the smooth rock.

Finally he backed away and came at the rock face in a lumbering rush. He tried the same tactics Sven had adopted; but though he was stronger than the young Mykines islander, he was also much heavier. He failed and fell back so heavily that he did not try again. Instead he began to prowl about the narrow strip of sand which ran like a sickle along the far wall of the Inlet. That was how he discovered the Chimney.

Sven, already suffering cramp in his legs, could almost guess what the animal was thinking. There was no way out of this prison except by climbing, and looking up the Chimney the bear must have seen the vague suggestion of sky above.

There was a steady flow of water coming down the Chimney, and that may have helped the bear decide to climb. Perhaps he had gone up small waterfalls back in Greenland. He squatted at the foot of the Chimney for perhaps two minutes, then ambled into it.

Sven's first impulse was to drop to the sand, race across to where his rope was snubbed, and the moment it was clear start climbing. He knew he could get back the way he had come, provided he chose a different starting point. Fear held him in check for a minute or so—fear that the bear might decide not to climb the Chimney after all. If he came out when Sven was on the sand, the end would be quick.

A minute passed with no sign of the creamy body. Another minute, and Sven could wait no longer. His leg muscles felt as if they were being twisted in the grip of giant pincers. He half turned and, his balance gone, leaped for the sand below.

He rolled over, scraped some skin from the palm

of his right hand on the sharp stones, but hardly felt the bite of it. Scrambling to his feet he freed his rope, raced back to the rock face, his eyes seeking a good place, and within ninety seconds of leaving his original perch was climbing from ledge to ledge, the free rope dangling below in a growing loop.

Not until he was thirty feet up did he pause to catch his breath. When he looked back the Inlet was still without life. The bear must be climbing the Chimney.

Only then did a dreadful thought occur to Sven. Up on top, not for a moment suspecting that the gallant swimmer from the schooner was other than a man, would be the women—his mother among them. There was also his Grandfather Napoleon, his Uncle Aksel . . . neither of them young men. And there were two other men even older still.

For seconds Sven was almost sick with horror at the thought of it. He could visualize the polar bear climbing out of the Chimney. In all probability no one would be looking in that direction. No doubt they would be watching the cliff, or watching the sea and the *Faroes Seeker*.

Sven began to climb. He took chances no fowler would normally take, clawing at niches which tore his finger tips. He should have climbed higher as he passed along the western wall of the Inlet, for the spray was bathing everything, making the rocks like glass; but he was in too desperate a hurry. He had to get out to a place where he could signal those above to begin to haul him up.

It was a race; a race in which he thought the bear had every advantage. It took a boy fifteen to twenty minutes to climb the Chimney, but Sven had no illusions about the climbing powers of a bear. Surely an animal like that could climb far quicker than even the most agile boy.

When he finally got around the corner of the Inlet to a position where he could tug on the rope and give those above the signal to hoist, Sven had to pause for a moment. His lungs were racked with pain, and his mouth was wide open in a desperate effort to get the air he needed.

He would have given anything for a few minutes' rest, if only to lean against the cliff while his tired muscles relaxed and the pain in his chest subsided a little. But he could not forget the bear. It would be scrambling up the Chimney, and every moment he waited spelled increased danger to the people on the cliff top.

He hauled in the slack and gave two quick jerks on the rope. After a moment or so the rope began to slide upward, and he let it run through his hands, putting a little tension on it so that when all the slack was taken up there would not be too much of a jerk for those on the other end.

When the rope did go taut he was swung off the ledge too quickly for his comfort. There were six women on the rope above, and like all the women-folk of the isolated Faroe Islands, they were almost as tough as the men. Theirs was a hard life, and from girlhood they were able to do things women in other lands could never do.

Sven was quickly hauled up the first hundred feet, and once again he sent clouds of sea birds whirling off their ledges in angry surprise. Many of them flew around him, diving in as if they meant to jab him with their beaks, only to wing away at the last moment.

There was no time to think of them, nor to wave them off. Sven had his work cut out keeping himself clear of the outjutting ledges. Then, when he was about sixty feet from the top, his progress halted—and the rope went so slack that he began to slither down. He grabbed at a ledge, found a foothold and hung on, waiting and wondering.

After a few moments he jerked on the slack rope to signify that those above could begin hauling again if they were ready. To his surprise he got four quick jerks in reply, then the rope went slack. For a minute he waited, expecting a signal from above, but nothing happened. Then, growing more and more worried, he hauled on the slack rope, intending to jerk it when it grew taut.

He drew in two feet, then another two feet, and still the rope remained slack. He hauled in more rope, but there was no resistance at all. Cautiously

he tugged and drew down almost a yard of rope—
that told him all he wanted to know, and confirmed
his worst fears. There was no one on the rope!

The truth hit him like a blow in the face. There
could only be one reason why the rope had been
left unattended: the bear had got to the top of the
Chimney! It was one of the unwritten laws in the
islands that a climber's rope was never left unattended except in the gravest of emergencies.

Sven stared upward and yelled; but the wind tore
his words away. He knew even as he shouted that
he would not be heard. In desperation he tried the
rope again, hoping against hope that someone
might have come back to it. There was no tension
on it at all. His cautionary tug merely brought
down another foot of slack.

For a few moments he leaned against the rock,
trying to think what he should do. If the polar bear
had got to the top, there was no telling what he
might do.

Sven shivered in terror as he conjured up a picture of the huge, creamy-colored beast smashing a
great paw down on his mother. It was that thought
which made him act. There was no point in worrying about the rope any longer. He untied it from
his waist and began a free climb.

Anxiety brought a dew of sweat to his forehead
and upper lip. In addition to his mother there was
his grandfather. Napoleon Berge was very fond of

saying he was as strong as, if not stronger than, many of the younger men. For a man of his years—he was over seventy—he was in fine condition; but he would never be able to outrun a starving polar bear. What was more, and this added to Sven's fears, he knew his mother would never run for safety and leave her father behind.

Sven climbed as he had never climbed before, though what he could do when he got to the cliff top he did not know. He just wanted to be there to stand by his mother and grandfather.

He was some fifteen feet from the top when to his amazement a shower of dirt came down on him. He stopped, shielded his eyes with one hand, then looked up. To his horror he saw a pair of feet sliding over the edge of the cliff—someone was starting down. Whoever it was had not bothered about the rope, for he was at least a yard away from it.

Sven yelled an angry warning; but instead of being raised, the feet slid even farther over the top. Then the legs came in sight.

"Get back!" Sven screamed. "Get back! I'm below! If you fall you'll knock me off! Get back!"

The legs waved for a moment in air, then slid even farther off the top. The owner of them was going to try a climb down, and Sven could see that there was no foothold at that point.

"Get back!" he screamed again, and began to climb.

6: The Bear's First Kill

On the cliff top a number of things had happened after Sven was lowered down on the rope. Napoleon Berge suggested to two of the women that they go along the coast to follow the course of the schooner. A bulge in the coast line now hid her from sight, but Napoleon feared she was moving nearer the cliffs. Though he did his best to hide his anxiety he was convinced it would not be long before the *Faroes Seeker* was driven ashore. The wind was beginning to subside, but was backing from northeast to southwest, and for any ship without engines, that could be fatal.

When the two women hurried off around the rim of the Inlet, Aksel came from the edge of the cliff with a suggestion.

"What do you think about me going down the Chimney, Napoleon?" he asked. "I could take a rope. If the man gets ashore alive, young Sven is going to need help."

Napoleon considered the matter for a moment, his frown deepening.

"If he is alive we can't possibly haul him up the cliff," Aksel pointed out. "You couldn't get him out of the Inlet that way; but we could get him up the Chimney."

"I know," Napoleon said impatiently. "I'm thinking about you. You can't go down the Chimney—have you forgotten your arm?"

"Of course not," Aksel growled. "But I've got two good legs and one good arm. I can get down and I can get up. We can't send a woman down."

"No," Napoleon agreed. "Well, if you think you can . . . we'll get a rope ready."

There was ample rope. In all there must have been over a thousand feet of fowling rope, for each of the ten women had brought a length of a hundred feet. Four of the pieces had been knotted together to lower Sven; working swiftly, Napoleon and Aksel knotted three more lengths together.

As a precaution against a fall Aksel tied the rope about his waist. Then he turned to his brother.

"If Sven has got the man down there, we'll signal you to haul his rope up over the cliff. As soon as the signal comes, put the women on my rope, and we'll haul the man up the Chimney. But remember, it must be a slow haul, because Sven and I will have to be behind him, easing him through the narrow places."

"You'll be teaching me how to gut fish next," Napoleon grunted, but there was a twinkle in his eyes. "Go on, and mind you don't fall. I don't want to have to haul you up by myself."

Aksel went over the lip and into the Chimney. In less than a minute he was soaked, for there had been considerable rain during the storm, and now the water was draining down from the island top.

He grunted in pain a few times when he found himself trying to use his stiff arm; but by the time he had gone down some fifty feet he was getting the knack of it, and was making steady progress with the use of only one arm and his feet.

At a hundred and twenty feet Aksel paused for a rest. It was then that he first heard the curious sound from below.

Usually there was very little noise in the Chimney. No wind could get in there, and the only sounds came from the waves as they broke on the stony bank at the bottom of the Inlet. Those sounds were always muted by the rock walls.

The noise Aksel heard made him frown in puzzlement, for it was a kind of animal grunt.

Wedging himself more firmly in the Chimney, he wriggled until he could look down past his feet. There was a vague kind of half-light in the tunnel, some of it coming from above, some of it from below, and by this time Aksel's eyes had become accustomed to the gloom.

He could see the way the Chimney wound, sometimes widening, sometimes almost closing shut where the rock stratum was of a more durable kind, and resistant to the action of water.

For several seconds there was nothing to be seen, but there were more of the queer grunting noises. Then, perhaps a dozen feet below, something came into view. If the bear had not been creamy in color he might well have blended in with the rocks; but his very lightness made him stand out sharply against the darker background.

Aksel stared, and blinked. In his early twenties he had been a regular voyager with the cod schooners to the icy waters of the Davis Straits, and like most of the seamen who fished off the western shores of Greenland he had seen polar bears.

He thought he recognized the creature below, but for a second or so it seemed crazy for anyone to believe that a polar bear could be coming up the Chimney. On Mykines there were not even mice. The only wildlife were the sea birds.

The bear gave another grunt as he hauled himself up past a narrow spot, and Aksel realized he was not seeing things. Then he remembered that there had been something strange about the "man" they had seen swimming ashore. Even from the cliff top his body had looked white.

Aksel turned and began to climb, jerking on the rope as a signal to his brother to start hauling.

There was no answer from above, however, for a few moments earlier Napoleon had moved nearer the cliff. The women there had just got a signal from Sven to start hauling.

Napoleon had a premonition of disaster. If his grandson was coming back up the cliff it must mean one of two things—either the swimmer had not reached the Inlet safely, or he was dead. In those moments of worry Napoleon forgot Aksel. He still held the slack of the rope in his left hand, but there was so much slack that when his brother gave an urgent jerk—signaling that he wished to be helped up the Chimney again—Napoleon never felt it.

In the Chimney Aksel was climbing as fast as he could. Twice he paused to get breath, but each time he hurried on as he realized the gray shape below was drawing nearer. The polar bear's paws were covered with a mat of hair and he had little difficulty in getting a grip on the wet rock. There were few places where the Chimney was really perpendicular, and Aksel Berge's fears increased as he realized he was being overtaken.

The last forty feet were an agony for him. Hampered by his stiff arm, he lost his lead foot by foot. If the bear had realized there was a man ahead, Aksel would probably have had no chance; the animal was not really hurrying.

Fear gave Aksel strength, but he was completely

worn out when he reached the top. Wet from head to foot, his coat covered with green slime from the rocks, he somehow crawled out of the Chimney, then sprawled face down on the ground.

No one was looking in his direction. The women on Sven's rope were hauling as vigorously as they could; two women were coiling the rope expertly as it came in. Napoleon was standing as close to the cliff edge as he dared, looking down and waiting for his grandson to come in sight.

It was Napoleon's mongrel dog Wulf which gave the alarm. He cantered across to Aksel, then barked. He went on barking until the two old men, standing on one side of the women, looked across and yelled as they recognized Aksel.

Napoleon joined the two men and they lifted Aksel to his feet. His face had a bluish look, and his mouth was open wide as he tried to get his breath.

"I said you shouldn't have gone down," Napoleon scolded. Then his voice became gentle, "All right, Aksel, take your time, take your time. Come on . . . take it easy."

Aksel made a tremendous effort to sit up as they laid him on a pile of coats. He lifted an arm, pointed vaguely toward the Chimney and gasped:

"A . . . bear . . . bear . . . in . . . the Chimney."

"What?" The three men spoke together, and turned to look toward the mouth of the Chimney. Then Napoleon, with a quick shake of his head to the other men, said soothingly, "Yes, all right, Aksel, don't worry . . . we'll see to it. Just lie down . . . rest. That's what you need . . . rest."

Rest was what Aksel wanted more than anything, but he realized from Napoleon's tone that he did not understand the danger. Gulping, he tried to speak again.

"There's a . . . bear . . . looks like a polar bear . . . it's coming up . . . the Chimney."

Again the three men looked, and this time there was no necessity for Aksel to repeat his warning, for the polar bear was coming into view.

One of the women coiling the rope was looking toward the Chimney at that moment, and she saw the big, creamy-colored beast climb out onto the top. He shook himself, sending water spurting everywhere from his thick fur. For the moment he was unaware of the eight women and the four men. The woman coiling rope screamed.

"A bear . . . a bear!"

Napoleon's dog rushed toward the polar bear, barking madly. The women on the rope looked around and stopped hauling. For perhaps five seconds they were so startled they did not move. Then one jumped to her feet and began to run. It was a panic move, and the panic spread to the others.

Only one woman hesitated, Maria Klakk, Sven's mother. She hung on to the rope long enough to give the signal for Sven to stay where he was. Then, as the bear turned and began to amble toward them, she rushed to her father, grabbed him by the arm, and began to hustle him away.

The other two old men were already retreating, at a shuffling gait which was pathetic by comparison with the measured amble of the bear. But the creature was puzzled and a little wary, for Napoleon's dog was dancing in front of him, snarling angrily, yet retreating all the time.

Napoleon shook his daughter's grip from his arm.

"Go on, Maria," he ordered gruffly. "I can't leave Aksel."

"Then I'll stay." Maria's voice was shaky with terror, but she refused to obey her father. "Tell the dog to drive it off."

"Wulf! At him, Wulf! Go on, at him!" Napoleon urged. "Get at him, boy!"

The dog was a mongrel, big like an Airedale, but with the shoulders and stance of a bull mastiff. How many breeds were mixed up in him no one would ever know; but like most mongrels his loyalty to his master was superb.

Though he had been barking defiantly and his hackles were up, his tail was down, a sign that he was scared. When Napoleon ordered him to "go in," however, a change came over him. His tail lifted, and instead of dancing about and yelping, he halted. Now his legs were stiff, as is the way of fighting dogs. He stood in front of the polar bear with his head thrust forward. His lips were drawn back in a ferocious, grinning snarl, and from deep in his throat came a continuous growling.

He looked more like a real wolf than a dog, and the bear halted, his eyes shifting from the dog to the little group of humans, then back to the dog again. Napoleon and Maria were trying to get Aksel Berge to his feet—Maria coaxing, Napoleon arguing fiercely when his younger brother insisted he could not move.

Four of the women were standing some fifty yards away, not wanting to abandon their friends, yet afraid to come nearer. The others were helping the two older men down the slope toward the distant village. For the moment no one was thinking of the *Faroes Seeker* . . . or of Sven.

Maria and Napoleon got Aksel to his feet, but it was obvious that if they were to get him away they would have to carry him. Some color was coming back to his leathery face, but he needed time to recover from the ordeal of coming up the Chimney.

"I can't do it, Napoleon," Aksel gasped. "It's no use. Maria, let me go. Help me to the edge of the cliff. He won't see me there." While Maria hesitated, Aksel gave an impatient jerk of his left arm and broke Napoleon's grip on it. In a sudden rage as Napoleon stooped to take hold of his arm again Aksel yelled: "Go on, you old fool! Do you want him to slaughter three of us?"

There were tears in Maria's eyes as she released Aksel's arm. Time was running out for them. She knew the dog would not be able to hold the bear at bay much longer.

"I'll be all right," Aksel insisted, starting to crawl toward the edge of the cliff. "Get going!"

Napoleon motioned his daughter to move, and he followed slowly, his gaze on his dog. Wulf was still holding the polar bear back, but the creature was now on his hind legs, swaying gently backward and forward, and grumbling, as if trying to make up his mind what to do.

Once, when he was barely full grown, he had been brought to bay by a small pack of Arctic wolves. It was toward the end of a very bitter winter when food had been more scarce than usual. The wolves had cornered him, and hunger had brought them to the point where even a polar bear was worth tackling to stave off their hunger pangs.

When the survivors of the pack finally fled, leaving three of their number staining the hard-packed snow with their blood, the bear had been so badly mauled that he had been forced to lie low for a week to give his wounds a chance to heal. It had been a painful lesson, and this dark-furred, snarling fury which refused to back away reminded the bear of it.

Wulf had already made several feint attacks, pretending to rush in, only to halt just out of reach of the bear's swinging right paw. A blow from that would have finished the battle at once.

Very reluctantly Napoleon moved away. Looking back for a moment, he saw Aksel crawling as unobtrusively as possible toward the edge of the cliff, where a slope might hide him. There was nothing Napoleon could do, yet he hated leaving Aksel behind . . . and he hated to see his dog face the bear alone.

Maria called to him, and the situation altered in seconds. As if deciding it might be easier to tackle the humans than the dog, the bear turned aside and started off after Napoleon.

Wulf gave a ferocious snarl, and with two stiff-legged leaps was barring the bear's path again. Even Napoleon realized that he dared not stay behind any longer, and quickened his pace. Maria took his hand as they followed the others toward the houses a mile and a half distant.

Aksel, now on hands and knees, crawled slowly to the cliff edge. The ground sloped for the last half-dozen yards before the edge was reached, and he was hoping that by lying flat near the brink he could remain unnoticed.

The lull between bear and dog came to an end. Wulf was still barring the way and the polar bear realized that the humans were moving off. His hunger was a fierce pain, and the snarling Wulf was too small to stop him for long.

The bear suddenly dropped on all fours and seemed about to retreat. Convinced he had frightened the big beast, Napoleon's dog rushed in. His eyes were like green jewels, and as the bear turned to meet him, Wulf leaped. He was making for the traditional nose grip which dogs over the centuries have used when dealing with larger animals.

Aksel was slithering backward now and he saw it all. He opened his mouth to yell a warning, but he was seconds too late. The bear half rose, his right forepaw dangling loosely. But as Wulf rushed in, the paw swept round so quickly it seemed no more than a blur.

Groaning, Aksel shut his eyes for a moment. When he opened them again a second or so later poor Wulf was spinning through the air. He had been stopped in his rush by a smashing blow on the side of the head. Wulf was dead before he even struck the ground.

Twice he rolled over, then slid over the brink of the Inlet and was gone. The polar bear, having swiveled around to be ready to finish off his foe if he came in again, stared in surprise, almost as if he suspected a trick. When the dog did not reappear, the bear ambled cautiously to the edge of the Inlet and peered down. His eyesight was not good, but his sense of smell was remarkable and he knew the dog had gone over the edge. For perhaps twenty seconds the bear remained sniffing at the rock, then whining as if cheated, he turned away.

Aksel had made good use of that short respite. His breathing was a little easier now, and he slithered backward toward the edge of the cliff. He was pinning his hopes on that slight dip in the ground leading to the cliff edge. If that failed him, there was no safe retreat. He would be cornered. Behind him was a drop of over two hundred feet to a raging fury of breaking waves, the spray leaping fifty feet into the air.

Though the wind was dropping quickly, it was still blowing from the sea over the cliff edge, and it was this which decided matters. The bear turned his back on the Inlet and for a few seconds stood testing the breeze, his black wet nose quivering. The breeze brought him the scent of man, and having got wind of Aksel, the bear started forward to investigate.

There was no time for deliberations. The animal was no more than thirty yards away, and though he appeared to move leisurely he covered the ground faster than a man could walk. Aksel had to do something quickly.

He inched backward until his knees were on the edge of the cliff and his feet in space. Then he yelled, hoping to startle the bear. For a moment it seemed as if he might succeed; but three days without food had given the bear such an appetite that no amount of strange sounds would make him forget it. His nose told him that nearby there was something alive and he came on again.

Aksel slid farther backward. There was no doubt what would happen if he was dragged back onto level ground. One blow had killed poor Wulf. One blow would kill him, too. He might die if he went over the cliff edge, but there was just a chance that he would be lucky and find a ledge with his feet.

The bear seemed to realize that his prey was disappearing in the same way that the dog had disappeared, and he rushed the last few yards. Aksel pushed desperately and dropped down over the edge of the cliff just as the bear came to a halt and, with right paw out, made a sweeping movement which would have pinned Aksel's head against the rocky rim had he still been there.

Aksel won that part of the race, but his widespread feet found no ledge to check his drop, and his clawing fingers did no more than break fingernails on the smooth rock as he fell.

7: Besieged Village

The cold wings of Death brushed Aksel's shoulders in the next moment, but as he slid downward something caught him in the small of the back, pressing him relentlessly against the rock, and at the same moment Sven yelled angrily, "Uncle, what are you doing?"

For several tense seconds it was touch and go whether Aksel's weight would push Sven off balance. Clambering upward at reckless speed, Sven had reached a footwide ledge no more than two yards from the top of the cliff when his uncle came slithering over.

Somehow Sven had got a hand up, slammed it into the small of Aksel's back, and, pressing him against the cliff, halted his downward rush. At first they teetered dangerously there, Sven almost losing his balance, Aksel too shaken to try to save himself.

Above them, and snarling in a fury of disappointment, the bear peered down and even swept a paw around in an effort to reach Aksel's head. It was then that Sven made good his boast that he could climb as well as any man. He shifted one foot an inch or so, giving himself a little better balance, and lifted his other hand up to steady his uncle even more.

Aksel, his wits coming back to him, raised his left hand, feeling for the least cranny in the rock which would ease his weight on his nephew. At last he found a crack.

"Hold it a moment, Uncle," Sven pleaded. Then, after a quick look, he added, "Put your left foot out—there's a little ledge about six inches from you. Farther—that's it."

While the bear stared down at them, his jaws wide open, the two islanders fought for their lives. Sven eased his uncle's right foot to one side, and a minute later both of them were on the wider ledge, leaning against the rock face, too spent to do anything but gasp for breath.

For ten minutes they remained there while the bear prowled backward and forward on the very rim of the cliff. Twice he lay down and reached so far over the cliff that he seemed in danger of losing his balance. The second time he did slip, and that must have shaken even his nerve, for he got back on all fours and disappeared from view.

Sven and his Uncle Aksel moved to safer positions. When a man had time to look, there were plenty of ledges on these cliffs, and for the moment they were in no real danger.

Sven wanted to know what had been happening, and Aksel's story of his climb down the Chimney, and the desperate race back for the top, made Sven's account of how he saw the bear come out of the water seem almost tame.

It was Aksel who finally suggested that his nephew work his way farther along the ledges, and then come up on top some distance away. If he did that, he would perhaps see where the bear was without the danger of coming face to face with him.

When Sven came out onto the cliff top there was no sign of the bear, and though he scrutinized the land for as far as he could see, no white blob broke the expanse of greenish brown moor. He hurriedly called Aksel, and swinging the rope which was still trailing over the cliff to within his uncle's reach, helped him up.

Sven suggested they ought to carry some of the rope back to the village, but Aksel would not hear of it. He had seen the bear in action, and knew that if they had to run for it, a rope, even only one of the 100-foot lengths, would have to be thrown away.

Aksel had almost recovered from his exhausting ordeal, and they alternately trotted and walked the distance to the village. When they got there it resembled an overturned ants' nest. Women and children were hurrying to and fro between the houses and the schoolroom, with Napoleon Berge acting as superintendent and watchdog. He had his old fowling piece tucked under his right arm, though such a weapon would be of little use against a polar bear.

Napoleon greeted the arrival of Sven and Aksel with a roar of delight, and grabbing his brother by the shoulders, gave him a shake to show his relief.

"I hated to leave you, Aksel—" he exclaimed.

"It was the only way," Aksel interrupted, turning to greet his wife, who was running toward them. After embracing her, he asked, "What about the bear? Have you seen it?"

"No!"

Then the mother of one of the young women who had been sent along the coast to see what happened to the *Faroes Seeker* pushed her way through the ring surrounding Aksel, Napoleon, and Sven. She wanted to know if they had seen her daughter.

"I sent her and Lisbet along the coast," Napoleon explained. "Anyway, now that you are back, Aksel, you can see to things here. I'll go and look for them."

"With that?" Aksel asked, pointing to the old fowling piece. "What use would that be against—"

"I won't even need it," Napoleon said. "The

polar bear is probably on the other side of the island."

"And if he isn't?" Aksel demanded.

"If he isn't I'll have to take a chance," Napoleon said grimly. "Look, I sent those two girls along the cliffs. I'm responsible, so I'll go and fetch them back."

"I'll come—"

"You'll not," Napoleon said, refusing Aksel's offer. "If you could have seen your face when you climbed out of the Chimney you wouldn't make such a crazy offer. I thought you were going to die."

"I'll come with you, Grandfather," Sven volunteered. "Who has another gun?" He looked from one anxious woman to another.

Five minutes later a gun had been brought out. It was not quite so old as Napoleon's ancient weapon, but it was only a fowling piece just the same. Against an animal with fur as thick as a polar bear's it would be practically useless.

"Be careful," Maria Klakk warned, but she made no attempt to stop her father and her son from going. When all the able-bodied younger men were off the island, then the pick of those who were left had to take charge. Sven and Napoleon were the pick—a sixteen-year-old boy and a grandfather who was well on in his seventies.

As they walked out of the village, preparations

were going ahead with haste to meet the situation. Napoleon had decided that it would be best for everyone to gather in the schoolroom. There they could help one another. If each family had to fetch its own water from the stream, it would mean people moving out into the open at different times; a source of danger if the bear happened to move down among the houses.

What was more, the women would feel better in a crowd; for there were one or two with babies, and no other members of the family at home.

Napoleon broached the matter of his dog when they got away from the houses, and the corners of his mouth drooped a little when Sven told him how Aksel had seen Wulf die.

"When we kill that bear I'll make his claws into a little memorial to the dog," Napoleon muttered. "You know, Sven, my boy, there is something about a dog you don't get from any other living creature. Wulf saved us all."

Sven glanced sideways at his grandfather. It was queer how the old man never seemed to have any doubts. He did not say "if" we kill the bear; he seemed to take it for granted that the bear would be killed. Yet Sven knew that if they came face to face with the creature, it would be almost a miracle if they succeeded in killing him with their antiquated guns.

They were half a mile from the village when over

to the left they heard the frantic baaing of sheep. Both stopped—so much bleating was unusual. There would be occasional baaing before a storm; but for the sheep to be bleating in chorus made Sven and his grandfather uneasy. Yet though they stared in the direction from which the sound was coming they could not see even one sheep.

"Should we go and look?" Sven asked.

"No, we've got to find those young women before the bear does! Come on!"

They had gone no more than fifty yards when the two young women came in sight. They were keeping as close to the cliff edge as possible, and one seemed to be pulling the other. Sven raced to meet them, and taking the free hand of the lagging one, helped her along. He asked no questions, for both women were panting heavily as if they had run the whole way from the far end of the island.

When they reached Napoleon he waved to them to slow down, and asked, "What about the schooner? Is she still afloat?"

For a moment neither girl answered; both had turned to stare up the slope toward the center of the island, for the bleating of sheep was even louder now. Napoleon repeated his question, adding, "There's nothing to be frightened of. Just keep walking and breathe deep."

"But there's something over there," one of the young women insisted between gasps for breath.

"We saw it. It is big and white and it is chasing the sheep all over the place. It can't be a dog—it's as big as a small horse."

"Oh, that," Napoleon said, and to Sven's amazement his grandfather managed a reassuring chuckle. "It's a bear, a polar bear, but it won't come near us. Anyway, don't bother about the schooner—you can tell us when we get back to the village."

The reason for his sudden change of mind was apparent at once. Over the top of a little hill half a dozen sheep had appeared, and they were racing toward the village as if a dozen fierce dogs were yapping at their heels.

Napoleon began to trot. The two girls, panting though they were, also broke into a trot. Converging on them from their right the sheep were soon joined by a score of others, then more, until it seemed as if all the sheep on the island had been rounded up.

They filled the air with their terrified bleating, and the reason for it was soon obvious. Over the rim of the rising ground came the polar bear. He was blowing hard, for Mykines sheep are as nimble as goats, and equally hardy.

For half an hour the bear had chased first one and then another, until their bleatings had got the whole wide-ranging flock on the move. Naturally they started off toward the village where, when wintry storms made life on the higher reaches of the island impossible, they were always given cover and food.

A grim race developed in the next few minutes, and Napoleon began to lag behind. His spirit was willing, but he could not keep up with the young women, even though they were winded from their long run.

"You go on!" Sven ordered the girls, and dropped back to keep pace with his grandfather. Without a word he took the fowling piece. Napoleon gave him a quick glance from beneath shaggy gray eyebrows, but did not waste breath in protest.

The first half-dozen sheep caught up with them when they were fifty yards from the nearest house. Sven yelled at them, afraid that if they jostled his grandfather, they might send the old man sprawling.

Behind them came a strung-out flock of almost a hundred sheep, with the lordly master of the flock, a big ram, running among the last dozen ewes. The sheep were spurred on by fear, the polar bear by hunger. He had never eaten a sheep, but the smell was making his mouth water; if he had not wasted so much wind and energy chasing first one sheep and then another during the past thirty minutes, he would probably have made a kill much earlier.

In the village there was a mad rush for safety

when the two young women came in sight, with Sven and Napoleon running some forty yards behind. No one needed to be told what was happening. Women screamed to children who were still carrying things from their homes to the schoolhouse.

In less than a minute everyone was indoors, and Maria Klakk was standing at the schoolhouse door, calling to the tired young women to come into the schoolhouse instead of their own homes.

By the time they had been helped indoors, the space between the little stream and the houses was filled with panic-stricken sheep. All seemed to have the same idea: to go to the house where they were cared for during the winter. Sven and his grandfather lost precious seconds when a terrified mob of half a dozen ewes turned away from one house and dashed across their path.

By this time the bear was in sight, chasing the slowest members of the flock. Sven and Napoleon staggered across to the schoolroom, were helped inside, then the door was slammed shut and the big wooden bar rammed into its sockets.

In the next half-minute tragedy came right up to the schoolhouse door.

The old ram was doing his best to keep the last few ewes ahead of him, but they sensed that their pursuer was gaining on them. One turned toward the schoolroom at the sound of the door slamming.

The others also turned. The ram, with a defiant bleat, raced on to head them away from the building as if he knew this move was a foolish one.

The closed door turned the sheep away, but they had lost precious yards and the bear made a final mighty effort to close the gap between him and a meal. The women and children watching from the windows of the big schoolroom held their breath for a moment when they saw what was coming.

The bear gathered himself for a final effort. In three huge bounds he cut down the gap between him and the little flock. It seemed as if a bomb exploded among the terrified ewes. They scattered, but one was left behind.

At a distance of no more than ten feet from the schoolhouse wall the bear made his kill. He slithered to a halt, and there was a pathetic bundle of ginger-colored wool under his right paw.

An eight-year-old boy at one of the windows screamed a protest. "Mother, that is one of our sheep! He has killed one of our sheep!"

He looked anxiously across at his mother as if expecting her to do something. Sheep were very valuable; but his mother, like the rest of the women, remained staring through the window. All kinds of hardships were endured by the people of Mykines, but the problem of a polar bear was something they had never experienced before. None of the women knew what to do.

The bear, his flanks heaving, looked around as if daring anyone to come near. He may have heard the boy's scream, for he glared directly at the schoolhouse windows. It made some of the mothers call their children down off the wooden seats.

Napoleon finally broke the paralysis which seemed to have gripped everyone. "Sven . . . my gun," he ordered.

Maria Klakk looked at her father, sudden fear showing in her eyes.

"Your gun! Father, you are not thinking of trying to kill the bear, are you?"

"Somebody's got to kill it," Napoleon said heavily. "What do you think will happen if we don't? Are we going to sit here while he eats sheep after sheep? In any case we've got to get out. Where are those two girls? What has happened to the schooner?"

Both young women were sitting with heads bent and shoulders heaving. At Napoleon's words one of them looked up. With a hand to her throat, she said, "It went on the ledges at East Cliff, Mr. Berge. Broadside on. The waves were breaking right over it."

There was a chorus of low groans at the news. On this small island there was not a man, woman, or child who did not know East Cliff. It towered some three hundred feet above a shallow half-moon bay. A scouring rip-tide had eaten away the cliffs, and even undercut them so that a huge cave ran in from the water for many feet. Great slabs of rock lay across the bay, like huge tables, and any vessel taken in by the tide could be written off as lost.

The second woman, more distressed than the one who had spoken, lifted her head to murmur, "Tell them . . . about the island boat!"

Heads turned at that, and some of the hopelessness left the eyes of the women who had relatives aboard the *Faroes Seeker*. Just before the schooner was swept into the East bay, the two watchers had seen a small vessel approaching which they took to be one of the interisland boats, a motor-driven vessel of some sixty tons.

"If they could get a line aboard the *Seeker*," Napoleon said, "the crew might be saved. Sven, give me that gun!"

There were protests from others besides Maria at the idea of Napoleon going out to face the bear. Those by the windows had been watching the way in which the dead ewe was being torn to pieces. The polar bear was obviously famished, and anyone who went out to try to finish him off would have to have a powerful rifle.

"All right, all right," Napoleon said angrily. "But there is one thing we must do. Somebody has got to get to the lighthouse. Christiansen will know what is happening. If the island boat the girls saw is from Thorshavn, it'll be in touch by radio with the lighthouse. If they can rescue the schooner's crew—that is fine. If they can't—then we've got to do something."

"But what can we do, Napoleon?" the oldest man on the island asked shakily. "I've seen polar bears when I was a young man, and you can't finish them off with a fowling piece. You must have a heavy rifle."

"I'm not thinking about the bear," Napoleon grunted. "I'm thinking about the men on the *Seeker*. Are we going to sit here while they drown? They won't give in without a fight. And I'll tell you something else . . ."

He paused and looked around the schoolroom. There were more than a score of women there, some in their early twenties, others ranging up to the sixties and seventies. Besides them there were perhaps twenty children, and two men older than Napoleon. All were silent, save for a baby which was crying sleepily.

Sven stood on one side and watched his grandfather proudly. Old he might be, but in this moment he was their leader.

"If I were on the *Seeker* right now," Napoleon went on quietly, "I would be saying to myself, 'Hang on, for the islanders won't let us die without a fight.' That's what I would be saying—and that's what my son-in-law will be saying. My son-in-law, Maria—your husband! If nobody else wants to go—I'll go to the lighthouse. We must find out what's going on."

Sven tiptoed to the nearest window and looked out. The bear was finishing off the ewe he had killed. There was not a lot of meat on the island sheep. Certainly not enough to satisfy a 1,000-pound polar bear which had eaten nothing for at least three days.

His heart missed a beat as he thought what might happen if he volunteered to go to the lighthouse, and was caught by this cream-colored killer. Yet he was the one who should go. He was the only teen-age boy on the island now.

Turning, he said, "I—I'll go, Grandfather. What do we want to know?"

There was an uncomfortable silence in the big room. Then Maria spoke:

"And I shall go with him. If there are two with guns it'll be less dangerous."

"A woman shouldn't go," Napoleon protested, twisting at his beard. "Maybe I should go. After all, I've seen my best days, and—"

"Father, you have already done more running about than is good for a man of your age," Maria said. "Give us some spare cartridges; Sven and I will go to the lighthouse."

"Look, Mother, I could go alone," Sven protested. "There's no need for you to risk—"

"There is every need," his mother said firmly. "If you go alone and anything happens . . . if the bear caught you, for instance, hours might pass before we knew. In that time—well, the men on the schooner would get no help, would they?"

"I'll go," Aksel said dourly. "This is no job for a woman, and—"

"Can you shoot a gun with only one good arm?" Maria asked, and shaking her head, gave him a quick smile. "No, Aksel, if there is going to be any danger I'm capable of meeting it. I can run. And if I have a bear on my heels I'll no doubt run faster than anybody."

"Go out by the back door," Napoleon said. "If there is any trouble, fire your guns."

"Come on, Sven," Maria said quietly.

"He's still worrying the sheep," one of the women called out, and with that reassurance Sven and his mother slipped quietly out through the back door of the schoolroom, leaving behind a huddle of scared children, and women who whispered anxiously together. Aksel Berge loaded the only other fowling piece there was in the place and laid it on the table. Then Napoleon called for someone to light the schoolroom stove and make coffee.

"A cup of coffee will put new heart in us all," he

said, smiling. "And don't all of you look as if the world has come to an end. Everything is going to be all right. I have a feeling here." And he tapped his chest.

8: Duel with the Bear

Fear for her husband and the rest of the men on the *Faroes Seeker* gave wings to Maria Klakk's feet. She was panting when they got to the little steel bridge which connected the two islands, but Sven had been amazed at his mother's speed.

A few sheep were still waiting near the bridge, while others went over one at a time, baaing nervously as they trod the sand and gravel which the storm had thrown up, making the passage difficult.

The rest of the flock were already on the steep grassy slope leading to the lighthouse, and as is the way of animals, they had already got over their fright. The bear was practically forgotten, and they were enjoying the grazing here, which was much more luxuriant than on their own rugged moorland.

A shout from half way up the hill halted Sven and his mother. Edvin Christiansen came puffing down to greet them; he was much too fat to hurry anywhere.

"If you are coming for news of the schooner, I have it!" he shouted. "She has run aground at East Cliff, but I have just heard by radio from an interisland boat that the crew have somehow got a line ashore. Isn't it wonderful?"

"A line ashore!" Maria closed her eyes for a moment in relief. "Thank God!"

"We were coming for help," Sven explained, and stopped as Christiansen shook his head dolefully.

"I won't be any use," he said, "and that idiot Arni slipped as he was coming down the ladder and he's sprained his ankle or something. What kind of help is needed?"

Maria told him about the polar bear and Edvin Christiansen's eyes widened, then narrowed as his forehead puckered in a frown of disbelief.

"Polar bear! Have you actually seen it? Where could a polar bear come from?"

"That doesn't matter," Maria said quietly. "We need a rifle. Have you got one?"

"Not one powerful enough to kill a polar bear."

"We must do something. The bear is finishing off a sheep outside the schoolhouse—and everybody is penned in the schoolroom."

"But they can't stay in the schoolroom," Christiansen muttered. "They—look, we'd better go up to the lighthouse. A polar bear! I just can't believe it!"

"Why do you think our sheep are here?" Sven asked, drawing the Dane's attention to the sheep which were grazing in the vicinity of the bridge.

There was no more talk as they climbed the hill, for it was a steep slope. Christiansen was winded when he showed them into his living room, and his wife did not even wait, but put the kettle on the gas stove at once. There was a time for question asking and a time for silence. This was a time for silence.

Her husband sat in the chair, his barrel chest heaving, and he did not speak until the coffee had been made and his wife was trying to persuade Maria and Sven to try some of her newly baked cakes.

Edvin took a cup of coffee and stirred it slowly. "Mrs. Klakk," he said at last, "I told you that we thought the *Seeker's* crew had managed to get a line ashore. The interisland boat gave us that news by radio. Unfortunately that is all the help they are likely to be able to give. They dare not go in close enough to try and fire a rocket line over the schooner. You know what the swell is like outside East Cliff bay."

Sven and his mother nodded. They knew well enough. Long Atlantic rollers marched in and broke in explosions of foam on the masses of fallen cliff which littered the shallow bay.

"I'll see if there is anything else to report," Christiansen said, and yelled to Arni, who was in the radio room.

The lighthouse keeper's assistant hobbled in a minute later with his message pad. His right foot was swathed in bandages holding in place a poultice of the herb, Lady's Mantle. On Mykines, where the nearest doctor was always at least two hours' sail distant, and might be days away if the weather was bad, the islanders had learned to make the best use of herbs which grew profusely on their salt-sprayed coast line. Lady's Mantle was one which had long been proved good for sprains.

"The island boat has been talking to the schooner by lamp," Arni said. "They are rigging up a rough sort of breeches buoy, but the crew must have help once they get ashore. The engineer is in bad shape, and all the men are very near exhaustion. They haven't had anything to eat except biscuits since the storm began."

"Keep in touch, Arni," Christiansen ordered. Turning to Mrs. Klakk, he said, "Somebody has got to go over to East Cliff at once. If you can get hot drinks, dry clothes, and food down to the crew, they may survive. But if they have to stay there for another twenty-four or thirty-six hours until the seas go down enough to allow a boat in . . . well . . ." He shrugged; no further words were necessary.

Sven's mother closed her eyes for a moment and her shoulders sagged. It was all very fine for this big blond lighthouse keeper to say a thing like that, but there was no starving bear sitting outside his window.

Sven voiced her thoughts, saying urgently, "What about the bear, Mr. Christiansen? You ought to see him. He's bigger than an island horse, and he's starving. If you'd watched him tearing that sheep to pieces you'd understand."

"He does understand," Mrs. Christiansen said soothingly. "It is just that he is so anxious for the crew of the schooner. You see there isn't anything we can do. He has been talking to Thorshavn by radio, asking advice, asking for help. But what help can they give? You know what the sea is like around here. If only there were airplanes that could fly over these seas, but there aren't—"

"All right, all right, Hanna, now don't get worked up," Christiansen admonished. Then he looked apologetically at Sven and his mother. "I am sorry if I did not seem to understand, but I have been almost sick with worry over this schooner. I have pestered Thorshavn as my wife just said, but they cannot do anything."

He got up and strode heavily back and forth; and there was a bitter tone in his voice. "When you think that out there—in America, Russia, England—scientists are doing all manner of wonderful things . . . they even send men into outer space—but when a ship is wrecked on this tiny island and men are in danger of dying, there is nothing they can do. I have said time and time again that we should have a helicopter at Thorshavn for emergencies like this. Always the answer is the same . . . a helicopter does not fly very high. The winds which sweep the islands and the water between the islands when the weather is bad make it too dangerous for helicopters. Too dangerous! But men are dying at—" He stopped and shook his head sadly.

"Can't you think of anything we can do to drive this bear away?" Maria Klakk seemed suddenly very calm, and perhaps it was the quietness of her voice after his own angry outburst which made Edvin Christiansen stand for a moment and stare at her.

"There must be something we can do," he said. "Men have dealt with wild animals before. Why they even train wild animals, and—" Suddenly he stopped.

"What is it, Edvin?" his wife asked.

"I have just remembered something," he replied, sitting down in his chair. "Many years ago, when I was only a very small boy, my parents took me to see a German circus. It was in Copenhagen. There were wild animals, and one of the acts was with a big maned lion from Africa. I do not remember what went wrong but suddenly the keeper was lying in the sawdust and the lion was nuzzling at his chest."

Mrs. Christiansen's face puckered into an expression of pain.

"People screamed and began to leave their seats," Christiansen went on. "For a few moments it was terrible. Then—and how they got into the big cage I do not know—two men were forcing the lion away from the keeper. Each man had an iron bar, and the end was glowing almost white hot. I used to wake up at nights for months afterward, dreaming about it. They forced the lion into a corner, and other men dragged the trainer to safety. It was an amazing thing."

"Yes, but how can that help Mrs. Klakk?" his wife asked when he lapsed into silence again.

"I am thinking," Christiansen said slowly. "That lion was terrified of the red-hot pokers. If we had something like them, the bear could be driven away."

"Red-hot pokers!" Sven said. "Where would we get things like that? It would take too long."

"I know . . . red-hot pokers would be no use here," Christiansen agreed. "Just be quiet for a minute while I think. If we can get something that would be the same as red-hot pokers, it might do the trick."

There followed a minute or so of silence, during

which the ticking of the little clock on a shelf above the big stove sounded loud and solemn. Finally Christiansen got to his feet, and there was a gleam in his eyes as he spoke to his wife.

"Hanna, I think I have the answer to our problem. Mrs. Klakk, be patient for a minute or so," he added.

Then he nodded to Sven and beckoned him to follow.

In a nearby storeroom Mr. Christiansen selected a plank, and to Sven's amazement got an axe and smashed the fine piece of Norwegian pine into half a dozen pieces, each about eight inches long.

"Knock the bristles off that broom!" he ordered, and while Sven was doing this, the lighthouse keeper grabbed a roll of baling wire from a hook in the wall. He took wire cutters from a drawer, and with pieces of wire proceeded to fasten the short lengths of timber around the top of the broom handle. Then he filled a can with paraffin and soaked the wood thoroughly.

"You see what I am doing?" he asked. "I am making a torch. A torch that will give off a bright light, lots of heat, and one that should burn for some time. Come on, we shall see if it works!" He led the way outside, calling on his wife and Sven's mother to witness the demonstration.

It took two matches to start the paraffin-soaked wood burning, for there was still a strong, gusty wind blowing over the edge of the cliffs on which the lighthouse stood. Once the paraffin caught fire, however, it roared into flames a yard long, and a black wisp of smoke was caught by the wind and set whirling across the island top.

Mr. Christiansen waved the torch wildly about, but as the wood grew hotter the paraffin began to vaporize, and the flames refused to be discouraged by the pluck of the wind.

"It will work!" Christiansen announced, and after trying to extinguish the flames by rolling the torch head in the wet grass, he tossed it away, where it flamed and spluttered, refusing to die out.

"I knew we would be able to do something," Mrs. Christiansen said excitedly. "Edvin has always been a man of ideas."

"This is no time for boasting," her husband said, and turning to Sven, told him to collect the wire cutters and the roll of wire. He went into another storeroom and came back with a five-gallon drum of paraffin.

"We have paraffin on the island," Maria Klakk said. "It will—"

"Have you five-gallon drums in the schoolhouse?" Christiansen asked. "No, I thought you wouldn't have. Now listen carefully, for I have had another idea. Instead of breaking up wood for the top of the torch, bind pieces of peat on the top. Peat will soak up more paraffin than wood, so the flames will last longer. If you make a few torches you should be able to keep the bear at a safe distance for hours. Long enough to get some food and clothing down to the schooner's crew. Think you can do it?"

"We *shall* do it!" Maria said with resolution. "And thank you for all you have done."

"Don't thank me—thank God," was the gruff retort. "I cannot remember when I thought of that Christmas circus. It had gone from my head completely until now. Is there anything else you need? Perhaps my gun would be better than that one." He indicated the old fowling piece which belonged to Napoleon. "I would be afraid to fire that. It looks old enough to be in a museum. I'll get mine for you."

Five minutes later Sven and his mother were starting down the hill.

The lighthouse keeper apologized for not coming with them. "I have never really thought much about my—my fatness," he said hesitantly, "but if I came with you and we met the bear—I think I should be more of a hindrance than a help."

"Sven and I will be quite all right," Maria Klakk assured him. "We came by the backs of the houses and we shall return that way."

In the schoolhouse everyone had settled down after Sven and his mother left. Women found places where they and their children could sleep if it became necessary for them to spend the night away from their own homes. Napoleon and Aksel remained by one of the windows, watching the polar bear.

When he had finished off the sheep he spent some time clawing at his mouth, trying to loosen some wool which had become stuck in his teeth. Then he ambled across to the stream which ran down the street and slaked his thirst. Several times he walked down toward the boat landing, but he always came back to stand staring at the schoolhouse, as if he knew the villagers were within.

At the end of forty minutes Napoleon suggested that Aksel should go to the back door and watch from there for the return of Maria and Sven. Napoleon was growing more and more uneasy as time went on. Like most Faroes men he had been a fisherman most of his life, and he knew how dangerous the waters by East Cliff were.

If the men on the schooner were to be saved, help must reach them at the earliest moment, and time was passing too quickly for his peace of mind. What was more, he did not like the way the bear kept wandering off. If he chose to walk down toward the boat landing when Maria and Sven were coming back, he would certainly see them.

Thinking to keep the bear occupied he took a

piece of *skerpikjot* (wind-dried mutton), which was a standby food among the islanders, and opening the door a few inches, he tossed it out toward the bear.

"Come on, it's good!" he called when the bear merely turned his head and for a few moments seemed disinclined to investigate. Then the animal got off his haunches and strolled across.

Napoleon expected him to gulp down the tidbit, which weighed at least three pounds, but he was disappointed. After drying in the cold clear air of the island for several months the mutton acquired a strong smell, as well as turning a rather offensive purply red.

The bear sniffed at the raw slab of mutton, then turned away. Had he not eaten fresh meat recently he might have devoured it at once and looked for more, but his highly sensitive nostrils made him turn away.

Sitting down, he began to crunch one of the clean-licked sheep bones, only to stop and lift his head as if he had heard something suspicious. At almost the same moment Aksel came back into the schoolroom to shout:

"They are coming—up the back way!"

Napoleon did not even turn his head as he called, "Warn them to watch out! I think the bear has heard them!"

Head up, the polar bear was sniffing. If he had

not heard the approach of Sven and his mother, his nostrils had picked up a scent which brought him to his feet. With his long snaky neck thrust out, he sniffed several times, then began to lope down toward the end of the schoolhouse.

Napoleon turned and yelled excitedly to Aksel.

"Tell them he's coming!" he ordered. Then he ran to the front door, opened it and looked out, to make sure where their enemy was going. To his horror he was just in time to see the polar bear swing around the end of the building and vanish from sight.

All activity in the schoolroom came to an abrupt stop while Napoleon lumbered across the room to grab their one remaining shotgun. As he picked it up Aksel burst into the room, shouting:

"He's got them! They—"

Then from outside came the sound of a shot, followed by another almost at once. Napoleon found some of his lost youth in the next few moments. He swept Aksel aside, plunged through into the small kitchen, and yanking the outer door open, stepped out. As he did so he heard a scream, and knew it was his daughter Maria.

Napoleon Berge had led a hard and often adventurous life. He had seen many terrible things and faced many dangers, but the sight which confronted him now blanched his cheeks.

His daughter had fallen and was trying to roll

over so as to get to her knees, while the polar bear was hurrying toward her, apparently quite unharmed by the two shots which had been fired.

Even as he stared, momentarily petrified, Napoleon saw Maria fall face down and a second later the bear was pinning her to the ground with one big forepaw, and snarling defiantly at Sven, standing only a few yards farther on.

9: All Torches Lit

When the bear had confronted Sven and his mother, only thirty yards separated them from the back door of the schoolhouse. As they moved out of the cover provided by the house next to the school, the polar bear had ambled into view.

Sven, growing weary from the weight of the drum of paraffin, was lagging a pace or so behind his mother. He had just changed the drum from his right hand to his left when the creamy figure came in sight. He was not so prepared for it as was his mother.

Maria had a roll of wire and the wire cutters in her left hand; Edvin Christiansen's shotgun was in her right hand. No word had passed between her and Sven since they said good-by to the lighthouse keeper. Maria's anxiety had grown with every step she took, and she was tensed almost to the breaking point when the bear came in sight. She had had a premonition that they would not get back to the schoolhouse unseen, and had been going over in her mind what she would do.

When she saw the big creamy-colored body she reacted within seconds. The wire and the cutters were dropped and she swung up the gun. She fired, and a pattern of cream-yellow specks appeared on the stonework of the schoolhouse as pellets chipped the surface.

At the same moment Maria stumbled backward, a scream of pain wrenched from her. She had made the mistake of not ramming the butt of the gun against her shoulder. The result was a staggering recoil which hit her shoulder with the force of a hammer.

Her finger tightened on the trigger and fired the second barrel even as she began to fall. Sven was hampered by the gun in his right hand, the paraffin in his left, and he tried to steady his mother without dropping either object.

When he did release the paraffin his mother was almost down, and he had lost his balance, so that he had to step over her to keep from falling across her.

As he staggered to one side he saw the bear rear up on his hind legs, then come stalking forward. Everything happened in a matter of seconds. Sven lifted his gun and squeezed the trigger—but nothing happened.

Aksel Berge had loaded the weapon, and as a

precaution against accidents had pushed the safety catch to the "on" position. Sven tried again and again to fire the gun, so shaken by the swiftness of events that he never gave a thought to the safety catch.

At the very last moment he leaped backward, and the bear dropped down on all fours. Maria Klakk, seeing how hopeless it was to get away, ceased trying to get to her feet and flopped face down, her hands going to the back of her neck to protect herself against the bear's strong white teeth.

From the doorway of the schoolhouse Napoleon Berge stood for a second or so, then began to run forward, lifting his gun for a shot. He knew that even heavy bird shot could do little but infuriate the bear, but he had to do something.

Then he realized his grandson was directly in the line of fire. A charge of shot would spread by the time it got to the bear, and pellets could blind a boy. The thick finger crooked on the trigger relaxed. Napoleon halted, his throat working convulsively.

It was at this juncture that Sven Klakk did something no one in their right senses would have dreamed of doing. Reversing his useless shotgun, and grabbing it by the barrel end, he rushed at the bear. He was not even thinking of danger. All he could see was that his mother was lying face down, and the bear had a paw on her shoulder. He had seen this same creature tear a sheep to pieces and he leaped in to prevent the same thing from happening to his mother.

"Sven!" Napoleon screeched, and Aksel Berge, who had followed his elder brother out, winced almost as if someone had thrown something at him. Both men saw the bear straighten up to meet the attack. Then they saw him swing one of his big paws around.

Sven crashed the butt of the shotgun against the bear's snaky, triangular head. With a deep woof of pain and anger the creature sank onto all fours. The butt of the gun, broken away from the metalwork, seemed to bounce into the air. But a moment later Sven smashed the remains of the gun against the side of the bear's head. In that instant the boy was berserk, like some old Norwegian Viking warrior.

It was a moment when anything could happen. Sven was taking the most dangerous risks, and yelling like a madman. The bear seemed momentarily bemused, and when Napoleon started to run, and fired his gun accidentally, it was the turning point in the thirty-second drama.

The bear swung to one side and scurried back the way he had come, leaving Sven to stare stupidly at the broken shotgun as his grandfather and Aksel rushed up. Then, remembering his mother, he dropped to his knees beside her, imploring her to tell him she was not hurt.

There were tears of pain in her eyes, for the recoil from the gun butt had been a savage one, but apart from that she had suffered no injury. Napoleon stalked in between the house and the school building, after hurriedly reloading his gun; but the bear had scurried up the street in the direction of open ground.

In five minutes they were all inside, and with them the drum of paraffin, the wire cutters and the precious roll of baling wire. Sven had to sit down, for the moment the doors were shut he began to tremble violently, and could not even hold the cup of coffee which was handed to him.

Surrounded by women his mother was weeping—the aftereffects of shock—and she was finally persuaded to lie down on an improvised bed.

Gradually Sven stopped trembling. He poured out the story of what was happening to the crew of the *Faroes Seeker*, and explained why they had brought the paraffin, the wire and the wire cutters.

"I have always said that Edvin Christiansen had a soft job," Aksel Berge commented, "but I'll agree now that he has earned his money. Torches are the answer. How many shall we need?"

"The more, the better," one of the two older men suggested. "It's like a fire, the bigger it is and—"

He stopped then, for Napoleon was shaking his head.

"Don't forget, Hendrik, we'll be nearly four miles from here, and we've got to carry everything. If everybody has a torch we'll need twice as much paraffin. What do you think, Aksel—six?"

Aksel looked around the room, for he was trying to decide who should come with them. They needed some of the strong, younger women for rope work; he had already decided that there was only one among them who could possibly go over East Cliff, and that was Sven.

"If only we had three or four of the younger men—" Aksel began.

"We're wasting time when you say things like that," Napoleon growled. "We are the only ones here, and it's up to us to do what must be done. Now, how many do you think should go?"

They decided to take eight of the younger women. That many would be needed to help carry the ropes, the paraffin, the torches, and the food. Napoleon took charge, telling the women to make coffee, strong coffee with lots of sugar in it.

Acting as guard he escorted an eleven-year-old girl to half a dozen of the houses to collect thermos flasks. That was one item from the civilized world which the fishermen had long learned to take with them on day fishing trips.

There was no sign of the bear, and spirits were

rising as preparations went ahead. Strips of the *skerpikjot* were wrapped up. It had a strong taste which few but the Faroes people could enjoy, but there was no doubting its food value. A man could put a strip of the stuff in his pocket, and cutting off a piece now and then, go a full day without losing his strength.

Sven had several of the women helping him to make torches. They broke the backs of three of the school desks—an act which made the school-teacher close her eyes for a second, though she made no protest. The strips of wood were an inch and a half thick, and were of straight grained pine. They split cleanly down the middle.

At the end of each length of wood Sven wired several pieces of peat. These were given an initial soaking in paraffin so that they would be ready in an emergency.

When the group was ready to start they were all heavily laden. In addition to the food and the necessary ropes—they were taking six 100-foot lengths of fowling rope—they carried dry clothing and one blanket.

Some of the women wanted the rescue party to take more blankets, but there was a limit to what they could carry, and carry swiftly. Maria's plea that she be allowed to come was turned down.

As they gathered around the back door she laid a hand on Sven's shoulder and said, "Be careful."

That was all, but the expression on her face told plainly enough what it meant to let her son go again, knowing he would be the one to swing over the cliffs. They were perhaps the most dangerous of any cliffs on the Mykines shores. The battering wintry seas had brought down many thousands of tons of rock, and the faces were almost sheer. No sea birds nested there, which was a measure of how perilous the cliffs were. There was never time for grass to grow on the ledges, for each winter saw the fall of more rock.

Napoleon realized the acuteness of his daughter's anxiety. He turned back as the others walked out and put an arm around her shoulders.

"Maria, there are twenty men depending on us . . . and one of them is Sven's father. They've got to be rescued; but we'll take care."

Maria nodded, and turned away so that neither her father nor her son should see her knuckle the tears from her eyes.

The party of eleven got to the top of East Cliff after a hard and a worrying forty minutes. They trotted fifty yards, then walked fifty yards, and it was Sven who led them the easiest way. Few of the women ever walked to the eastern tip of the island, and only if sheep strayed there did the boys venture so far.

The ground was rough. There were stretches where the soil was so thin that a shoe could scrape it clear off the rock beneath. There were other places where for centuries water had seeped into hollows which had gradually grown over with reeds. These spots were dangerous, since many of the hollows were a score of feet deep; if a man fell into one he could be suffocated in the thick slime from which the reeds grew.

There were other patches where the ground looked quite firm, with grass growing on little islands of peaty turf. Brown-colored water ran between the reedy patches.

When they reached East Cliff, packs were dropped and everyone went to the edge of the cliff to see what was happening below. It was only noon, after a morning which had seemed like an eternity. The sea was still rolling in, the breakers advancing with the regularity of soldiers on parade.

Out to sea, no more than four hundred yards from the foot of the cliffs, the interisland boat was cruising slowly east and then west, and always sitting in a bath of foam. Her crew were taking a battering, but remained standing by just in case they could do something. They dared not come closer, for the broken water nearer the foot of the cliffs told its own story of massive slabs of rock lying just beneath the surface.

The *Faroes Seeker*, looking like a toy boat, was lying on her side. The waves had hurled her onto one of the big ledges, and with the tide now receding, she was firmly wedged there. Waves broke over her continuously, but the thing which brought cries of joy from the watchers on the cliff was the line—like a thread from a spider's web—which stretched from the wheelhouse to a point unseen at the foot of the cliff.

"It goes into the cave, Grandfather," Sven whispered. "I wonder if they all got ashore?"

"We'll not know until you've been down," Napoleon said. "Come on, we're wasting time."

They had brought a sack of peat with them, and a kettle, as well as a big can of water. One of the women lit a fire of peat and prepared to boil water for more coffee. The others helped to lay out the ropes while Sven, Napoleon, and his Uncle Aksel prepared a pack. They had decided that if it was humanly possible, the injured man must be hauled up.

Sven would take coffee and food down, and the blanket. It would be used to wrap the injured man in, so that he would have at least some protection when he was hauled up. Napoleon and Aksel had considered bringing Sven up with the injured man, to fend him off the rock face, but had decided it was too risky and more than they could manage.

They were almost ready to lower Sven when Napoleon saw something moving a little farther down the coast. Despite his years his eyesight was still good, and after a moment or so he knew he had not been mistaken. That light-colored form was the polar bear, and it was coming along the same route they had taken. Obviously it was following their scent.

Napoleon drew his brother aside. "What are we going to do, Aksel? The bear is coming. Don't look at once—I don't want them all to know."

But a moment or so later Sven came across to say, "Grandfather, have you seen the bear? He's coming."

"Well?" There was a challenge in the old man's voice.

Sven shrugged. "I just thought I'd tell you," he said.

A few moments later one of the women at the fire saw the enemy. Then all eyes were turned toward Napoleon.

"All right," he said defiantly. "It's coming, and we knew it might. That's why we brought the torches. What do you want to do? Huddle together and cry, or are we going to try and rescue the schooner's crew?"

"I think we should light the torches," one of the women said, coolly sitting down and making herself comfortable. "Are you ready to go down, Sven?"

Sven wriggled into the crude pack which they had constructed. It was heavy and cumbersome, with the blanket wrapped about the vacuum flasks to minimize the risk of breakage.

The other women chosen for the work of lowering Sven sat down on the damp turf and moistened their palms. One of the women at the fire unscrewed the top of the paraffin drum and began to splash paraffin liberally on the torch heads.

"All right, over you go," Napoleon said, and winked as he added, "By the time you get back we'll have singed this fellow's whiskers for him." He sounded so confident that Sven had to grin as he walked across to the cliff top.

He tied the rope end around his waist, but there was no question of going over the cliff edge. The women who should have lowered him were now on their knees, watching the bear as he ambled steadily up the slight slope. There was something ominously purposeful about the animal, as if he already knew what the end of it all would be.

Napoleon grabbed the first torch the moment its peat had been soaked in paraffin. He jabbed it into the fire and brought it out before it had time to flame. Muttering angrily he pushed it back again, and a few moments later was moving off to meet the bear.

Aksel followed his example, calling to his brother not to be in such a hurry. Napoleon stopped some thirty yards from the fire and the two men stood with their torches ready. For the first time the bear seemed as if he might be having second thoughts. He slowed and then rose to his full height, forepaws waving a little as if to help his balance.

"You come up here and you'll get more than you want!" Napoleon roared, and waved his torch in a figure of eight, a maneuver which produced a crossed ring of black smoke. He also sent blobs of flaming paraffin spurting around, for the peat had been very generously soaked.

The bear dropped gently onto all fours and came on again. One of the women was bringing another torch for Napoleon, but he shook his head, telling her to stand in line with him and Aksel. She had not expected that and for a moment looked flustered. Then she stepped to one side and stood by Aksel Berge.

It was a moment of growing tension, with all eyes on the bear. Would he be halted by the flaming torches, or would he just charge blindly on?

"Get back!" Napoleon suddenly roared, and started forward, his torch thrust toward the bear's head. Aksel followed his example, with the woman a foot to the rear. For her this was one of the worst moments of her life, and her face was gray with fear. Had she turned and fled she might have thrown the battle to the winds; but, though she was trembling, she kept her place.

When no more than ten feet separated them the

bear stopped, and Napoleon stopped. The old man stood just over six feet, but the bear seemed to tower above him. For fateful seconds they faced each other. A lunge on the part of the big, cream-colored beast could have gained him victory—he was too big and powerful for the strongest man to have withstood his charge; but he hesitated.

Napoleon suddenly gave a yell and leaped forward a full yard. His torch threw a faint red light on the bear—and the battle was won. Dropping on all fours, the huge beast turned aside.

10: The Defenses
   Crack

Suddenly showing a burst of speed, the polar bear tried to outflank the line of three torchbearers, but Napoleon was equal to the occasion. He, too, showed a turn of speed and, with Aksel on one side of him and the woman on the other, foiled the creature's attempt to get around their flank. Sulkily the bear stopped and sat down.

Napoleon, now confident of victory, turned and yelled to Sven:

"All right, over you go. We can deal with him. There won't be any trouble."

If Sven had hesitated, the women manning the rope might not have returned to their places, for they were not so confident as Napoleon appeared to be. But when it became obvious Sven was going to slide over the cliff top they dropped into line and grabbed hold of the rope.

Sven took a last quick look at the bear, then got to his knees and slid over the ledge.

The journey down was far more frightening than any he had ever made before. There were no sea birds to mob him, for this stretch of cliff was new. Less than a year before a great part of it had been so undercut by the swirling tide race that it had finally fallen.

As a result there were no ledges on which his feet could touch to steady his descent. The rock face was sheer, and in many places sloped inward a little, so that for much of the time he had difficulty in even touching the rock and swung completely free.

The wind which had been howling so wildly for the past three days had fallen to no more than a stiff breeze, but it eddied along the cliff, plucking at him and causing him to swing. Some of the small outjutting pieces of rock had sharp edges, and as he heard his rope scraping against them his anxiety increased. Island ropes were good ropes, for men's lives depended on them, but no rope could last long scraping continuously across hard rock.

When he had gone about a hundred and fifty feet he began to feel the soft dampness of spray, and when he went still farther down, the cliff face was glistening wet, and occasionally blobs of spume sailed past.

He began to look down past his right shoulder, ready to give a jerk on his signal rope. He was bringing down a second rope, which was being paid out along with the one on which he hung. The second rope was Aksel's idea. It was to serve first of all as a signal rope, and when Sven got to the bottom the two ends would be tied together to make one continuous rope. If they were to attempt to haul an injured man up the rocky face, a rope from below would be vital to steady him, since he would certainly not be able to help himself.

When he was no more than fifty feet from the cliff bottom Sven signaled those above to stop lowering. Clinging precariously to the rock face with one hand, he looked down and his hopes grew.

The tide was going out, but even more important was the position of the schooner. She lay parallel to the cliffs and was firmly wedged on a stretch of slightly tilted rock. In that position she was acting as a breakwater to the sea. The waves were bursting into huge masses of foam about her, but between her and the land the water was relatively calm.

Sven signaled for lowering to continue, and three minutes later he was standing at the foot of the cliffs. Water surged around him to knee depth, but because of the shelter afforded by the schooner he was in no danger.

Tying the ends of his two ropes to an outjutting nub of rock, he made his way slowly to the east, and rounding a rocky outcrop, saw the schooner's crew.

The men were huddled together in a very shallow cave, and he was within a dozen yards of them before they saw him. His father and the third mate came to meet him, staggering like drunken men. Their faces were gray with fatigue, their clothes sodden, and their hair was plastered down on their uncovered heads.

His father clasped Sven and held him tight. It was a moment or so before the boy could speak.

As they turned to walk toward the rest of the crew the men began to move, and weak voices were raised in a barely audible cheer. Sven dumped his heavy pack and carefully unrolled the blanket guarding the four big vacuum flasks. There were six pints of scalding hot coffee to be divided between a crew of nineteen men and the ship's boy. But one man was unable to enjoy his share—the ship's engineer, who was unconscious.

While he was pouring the coffee, and handing it out to men whose fingers were so stiff from cold that they had to use two hands to grasp the cup, Sven gave them the news. Some of the animation faded from the faces of the men when they heard that most of the people who could have helped in a rescue were off the island, having followed a school of *grind* over to Vagar.

"It doesn't make much difference anyway," Sven said, "for I don't think we could get you up the cliff. We—"

"You've got to get Olsen up," his father insisted. "If he isn't given warmth quickly he'll die. Look at him. You've got to get him to the top, Sven. Even if you stay, he's got to go."

Sven nodded. "We could haul one up, I'm sure," he agreed. "But the ropes won't stand much wear. This cliff face, Father, is just a mass of rough edges." He decided to say nothing about the polar bear; the crew already had enough worries.

When the coffee was drunk he handed out the strips of *skerpikjot*. However unappetizing it looked, the men ate as only famished men will, and at the same time began to strip off their sodden clothes. Sven had brought twenty woolen pullovers. They were thick, hand-knitted garments, and would keep the dampness from the men's bodies for a few hours at least.

By the time the men were dressed again they were more cheerful, even though all knew that they could not hope for rescue for at least another day.

The injured Olsen was carefully wrapped in the thick, homespun blanket. His head was padded with his own coat, then he was carried to where the two ropes hung down from the cliff.

One rope was tied about his waist, the other was tied about his feet. If he could be kept in an upright position as he was drawn to the top, there was less risk of injury from striking the rock.

Sven finally jerked on the signal rope, and a few

moments later the rope tightened and Olsen began to rise slowly. Sven moved as far away from the foot of the cliff as possible, keeping his end of the rope taut and thus holding the injured man off the rock face. Twice there was an agonizing halt when the rope wedged itself in a crack, and Olsen had to be hauled down until the rope was worked clear. By the time he was safely on top the journey had taken practically half an hour.

Three jerks on the rope told Sven that he could now be hauled up, and he turned to his father, suggesting that he should go.

"It won't be safe to haul anybody else up," Sven pointed out. "Look how the rope is fuzzing. The rocks haven't been weathered at all, and the edges are sharp. If you could—" And there he stopped, for his father was shaking his head, slowly but definitely.

"For the moment, Sven, I am taking the place of the captain," he explained. "Captain Neilsen is too weak to command. You wouldn't have me leave the crew in such circumstances, would you? No, you get up there; you can lower more food and dry clothes. The rope should stand light weights and we'll keep somebody down here, waiting for supplies. Give your mother a kiss for me." He clapped Sven on the shoulder and smiled. "Tomorrow we'll all be together again. Now, up you go."

Sven knotted the rope about his waist and gave

the signal to haul. For a few seconds there was no response, then the rope tightened suddenly and he was jerked off his feet. In the next few seconds he was fortunate not to have his skull cracked against the rock face, for he was hauled up at a breathtaking speed, far quicker than seemed possible.

When he did recover his poise he thought for a moment that there must have been unexpected reinforcements at the cliff top. Perhaps more of the island women had arrived. His spirits lifted at the thought, for if they had, they would surely have brought more dry clothes, more food, perhaps even blankets.

That was as far as he got in his thinking, for he had to fight hard to keep off the rock, and to keep from spinning about. He went up very quickly until he was about forty feet from the top. Then without warning the upward rush ceased, and for a moment he thought he was going to be plunged down to the bottom again. He began to drop, went down half a dozen feet, then was halted with a jerk which brought a grunt from him.

He looked up, wondering what had happened, and waiting for the upward haul to start again; but it did not.

On the cliff top the guard duty of Napoleon, Aksel, and one of the women had continued without trouble for almost half an hour.

The woman alternated between standing with the two men, a flaming torch in her hand, and going back to the fire to bring fresh torches newly soaked in paraffin when the torches they held began to burn low.

The polar bear tried several times to outflank the three guards, but when he padded quickly toward the cliffs the torchbearers followed him, always barring the way.

The bear whined and grumbled, and ambled this way and that. He would sit down to stare at the islanders for a few minutes, only to resume his pacing to and fro, like a bored tiger behind the bars of a zoo cage. Once he even turned and began to walk away, but he did not go more than fifty yards before he changed his mind and came back.

Then the women on the rope called out that they had gotten the signal to hoist. It had been agreed that if possible the injured engineer should be hauled up, and Sven had given the required number of tugs on the rope which indicated the engineer was coming up.

It was not until the injured man was almost in sight of safety that they had the first indication of a totally unexpected danger. The woman who had been resoaking the torches handed two fresh ones to the "runner," and as she did so whispered, "Tell Mr. Berge that there is almost no paraffin left."

The idea that they could use five gallons of paraffin in little more than an hour had not occurred to anyone. The drum had seemed a big one, and when Napoleon and Aksel got the news that probably only two more dippings of torches would be possible, it brought immediate concern.

Just then Napoleon was told that the injured man was safe. He assigned the woman who had been keeping the sacking under the rope at the point where it slid over the cliff edge to look after him. Then he told the women on the rope that they must haul Sven up as quickly as possible.

"It won't be long before the torches burn out," he warned, "and I don't want him half way up the cliff when the bear realizes that we can't keep him off any longer."

The five women exchanged glances. Like every woman on Mykines, these young women knew what it was to gut fish almost every day, and also salt them. Rubbing coarse salt into flaked cod and saithe toughened the hands, but even so the hands of these five were already showing the effects of hauling on the hard hemp ropes.

They all had ridged skin on their palms; one or two had blisters.

"We'll just have to rush it and forget the blisters," one of them said. "If the polar bear does come we can't sit here, and we don't want to leave the rope with Sven half way between sea and sky.

As soon as we get the signal we'll hoist, and no stopping."

The first four women did the hauling, the fifth had the task of clearing the rope behind her as it came in. They got the signal from below, and with the fifth woman chanting to keep in time, the "rush haul" began. No trained boat crew could have worked in better rhythm. The women swayed gracefully from side to side as they heaved first with the right hand, then with the left.

Before half the haul was done, two of the women were clenching their teeth against the pain of blisters which had formed and been broken in a matter of seconds. Still they went on, for there had been a warning shout from Napoleon that the last torches were showing signs of burning out.

"Get him up, girls!" Napoleon bellowed. "I can hold the bear only a few more minutes!"

That was why Sven shot upward so quickly, and so close to the top, before dropping abruptly down again. The drop came because one of the young women suddenly collapsed.

With a low moan she released her grip on the rope and fell sideways. Her fall put the woman behind her off stroke. She instinctively let go of the rope to grab at the fainting woman. The loss of two haulers at the same moment stopped the work, and for a second the rope ran out as blistered palms were eased off the hemp line which had suddenly taken on greater strain.

"Hold it! Hold it!" the front hauler screamed, and at once two of her companions grabbed and checked Sven's downward rush.

"What's the matter?" Napoleon yelled, not daring to take his eyes off the bear. In the past few minutes the animal had grown increasingly restive, as if he were trying to make up his mind to break this deadlock.

The two women who were trying to revive Olsen by the little peat fire left him and hurried across when they saw that one of the rope team had collapsed.

They stared in horror at the blistered hands of their friends. Swiftly they got into the line, taking the places of the two whose hands were worst affected. The woman who had been on the cliff edge also came to give a hand with the hauling.

"Is he up?" Napoleon yelled impatiently. "What's going on? Get him up—our torches are burning out!"

No one bothered to answer. It was a situation where shouts and commands were not needed. These island women had a hardihood bred through long years of battling with the sea and loneliness. They did not crack easily; nor did they panic at the first threat of danger.

They began to haul steadily, and not so quickly

as before, while the four who had heaved Sven up two hundred and sixty feet so quickly stood on one side, clasping their pain-racked hands. There was nothing they could do now but watch and hope.

Napoleon and Aksel were dividing their attention between the polar bear and the ends of their torches. The peat was now beginning to disintegrate. The paraffin was burned out of it, and the glow at the end could only be maintained by waving the torches to and fro. The keen air was blowing the peat to life, but at the same time eating it down to a fine white ash, which began to drop in large flakes at each change of motion.

"Where's Sven?" Napoleon bawled again. "Tell him to bring my gun!"

It was that yell which greeted Sven as he was hauled over the last few feet of slope from the cliff onto the level top. He was panting, for even though he had been taking as much of his weight as possible on his hands, the loop about his waist had gradually worked up until it was round his ribs, and the pressure had made breathing difficult.

For a few moments he lay sprawled on the thin turf, gasping and taking in the scene. He had not expected what he saw. Four panting women in a close group; one woman kneeling by another lying on the ground. Two women attending to Olsen; his grandfather and uncle slowly backing away as the polar bear advanced.

At first he could not understand why the two men were allowing the bear to drive them backward. Then he realized the danger. Aksel's torch was no more than a slightly glowing mass of collapsing peat on the end of a burning stick. His grandfather's torch was a little better, but the flames were dimming as the last of the paraffin burned out of the peat blocks.

Painfully Sven got to his feet. He stumbled across to the fire and picked up the shotgun. Napoleon did not know his grandson had been hauled up, and yelled again to the women to hurry up, and for one of them to bring his gun.

"I'm coming!" Sven shouted, and with a last glance at Olsen, who seemed to be showing signs of returning consciousness as the peat fire warmed him, he hurried across to his uncle and grandfather.

"You've been a long time!" Napoleon said crossly. "Here—take the torch! Give me the gun!"

Sven obeyed, at the same time asking, "What are you going to do?"

"Do!" Napoleon bellowed angrily. "I'm going to shoot the bear—that's what I'm going to do! When I say 'Ready' I want you to walk up with me—keep the torch pointing straight at his head. He'll rise on-to his hind legs, and then I'm going to jump in and shoot him in the heart."

Even as he was talking they were being forced

back. With Aksel's torch more or less extinguished, and the one Sven held rapidly dying down to a red glow of hollow peat blocks, the bear was growing bolder and walking slowly but deliberately toward them. It was almost as if he had decided to call their bluff.

"Look, Napoleon," Aksel pleaded, "you can't do it. You should have seen what he did to your dog. Wulf tried to get in close, and he could move much quicker than—"

"Are you ready, Sven?" Napoleon asked. "All right . . . now!" And lifting the gun he stepped forward.

11: Race for Survival

Napoleon Berge had no illusions about what might happen. "God help me to get my shot in," he whispered as the bear rose to his full height, presenting a picture to terrify the bravest of men.

It was then, as Napoleon lifted his gun, meaning to lunge in and try to get close enough for a shot which would put the bear out of action, that Aksel's nerve cracked. He had seen how Wulf had been killed, and grabbing Napoleon's arm he tried to jerk him back, yelling frantically, "You crazy fool, Napole . . ."

The rest of Aksel's words were drowned by the sudden thunder of the gun. Napoleon's finger had been crooked about the trigger, and the grab at his arm had made him tighten it.

As the charge of bird shot whistled through the air, well above the bear's head, the recoil from the gun, plus Aksel's pull, swung the old man around and threw him off balance.

Down went the gun as Napoleon tried to keep from falling. Startled by the roar, the bear backed away a pace or two, and might have turned tail had there been anything to follow up that first shot. Instead he saw Napoleon trying to get his balance, and Aksel desperately doing what he could to help him to his feet.

The bear changed his mind about retreat and lunged forward. His eyes were glowing green. He was desperately hungry, and a quick blow now would ensure a satisfying meal.

It was Sven who acted as the buffer. He had cringed back a little when the gun roared, and it was an instinctive act to step forward and thrust the dying torch into the gap when the bear moved in to make his kill.

If Sven's act was instinctive, that of the bear was, too. As the glowing peat came within range of his eyes, he did two things automatically. He halted his forward movement, swayed the upper part of his body back like a clever boxer, and at the same time brought his left forepaw around in a vicious, sweeping blow. It was the same kind of blow which had crushed poor Wulf's skull.

This time the victim was not flesh and blood, but the charring remains of several peat blocks, already burned to little more than empty shells. The blow sent glowing peat scattering in all directions; some of it onto the bear's own chest and head.

If Sven had not been gripping the other end of the torch so firmly, what followed might have been very different. Instead of the torch being swept out of his grasp, he was swung violently sideways, and reeled yards away as he struggled frantically to keep on his feet.

The bear was grunting in pain and anger while he pawed at his chest and the singed fur about his eyes. Had there been anyone to pick up the shotgun it would have been relatively easy to get within point-blank range. Sparks from the glowing peat had showered the bear and momentarily confused him.

To add to his bewilderment the women who a few moments before had been sitting gasping for breath were now on their feet. With no weapons at all they came racing across, screaming shrilly.

Sven recovered his balance and turned swiftly to see what was happening. He was ready to run, sure the bear would be coming toward him. He saw Aksel get Napoleon to his feet. Then he saw the women rush up, hands outstretched to help the two men, and in that moment the bear dropped on all fours and turned away—coming straight toward him.

Sven knew he had to run or die, for the bear was moving quickly. It was a moment for quick thinking. If he ran toward the clustered women he might well save himself; but he might also bring disaster to one of the women or the men. If he ran westward toward the village he could perhaps draw the bear away, and so leave his grandfather, Uncle Aksel, and the women to get on with the work of rescuing the crew of the *Faroes Seeker*—or at least get more food and clothing to them.

The choice was clear, and Sven realized what he must do. He turned to run west, and the polar bear followed him.

"He's going!" One of the women shouted, and for a few seconds no one spoke and no one moved. Napoleon had been hauled to his feet and was gently rubbing his right shoulder where the butt of the shotgun had kicked him.

Aksel stooped to pick up the shotgun. A thin feather of blue-gray smoke was still drifting from the right muzzle. He looked up at his brother and said apologetically, "If you'd gone in at him, he'd have killed you. You've no idea how quick he is. I saw him kill Wulf!"

Napoleon took the gun. He was staring down the greenish brown slope. The bear was now only a gray-white blob, growing smaller as he raced away. Ahead of him, also growing smaller, was another figure, less easily seen because the color of his clothes blended with the background. That second figure was Sven.

"What are we going to do?" one of the women

asked, her voice quivering. Though she did not address Napoleon by name, everyone looked at him for an answer.

"Where is he now?" he asked. He could see the bear, but not Sven.

One woman opened her mouth as if to answer, then lifted a hand to her lips in sudden dismay. Her sharp eyes could see what was happening with painful clarity. The bear had been slowly overtaking Sven, though he still appeared to have a lead of some thirty yards when they reached the bottom of the long, gentle slope.

Then came the change. The uphill grade of the land was an immediate advantage to the polar bear. With his forelegs shorter than his hind legs a bear runs less easily downhill. But uphill his longer hind legs are a decided asset.

"Well?" Napoleon roared. "What's happening? I can't see either of them now! Who can see them?"

He turned to Aksel, who shook his head. Two of the women suddenly turned away as if they had just witnessed something terrible, and Napoleon caught one of them by the arm. He shook her angrily, demanding:

"What has happened? Tell me! TELL ME!"

"I don't know!" The woman shook off Napoleon's grip, and tears were flooding into her eyes as she added, "I think he was caught. It seemed as if he fell . . . then you couldn't see either of them."

For a few moments even Napoleon was silenced. He stood there with his left hand clawing at his beard, the shotgun in his right hand. His throat worked convulsively as if he were choking on something. Then he gave a sigh and hefted the gun until it lay across the crook of his left arm. He broke it, tossed the spent cartridge away and reloaded.

When he finally spoke, his voice was curiously flat.

"Aksel, you had better try and get the rest of the food and the clothing down to the men below. Then send for more coffee, more clothing . . . blankets. You've got to keep them alive until tomorrow. Get some peat down to them—and paraffin. A good fire would help them."

"What—what are you going to do?" Aksel asked, his voice very low.

"I'm going to kill that bear!" Napoleon told him, and now his shoulders straightened. "I ought to have done it when he was eating the sheep. I could have got near enough then. If I can get rid of him now, at least Sven won't have died for nothing."

Aksel half opened his mouth as if to protest, but closed it without speaking. He knew his brother too well to waste words now. Napoleon had made up his mind and nothing would turn him aside.

"If I don't see you again, good-by, everybody." Without another word the old man started to walk down the slope. For perhaps half a minute no one moved or spoke, then Aksel said:

"I think we'd better get the rest of the supplies baled up in the blanket. The sooner we get them lowered, the sooner we can get Mr. Olsen carried down to the village, and bring up more food and dry clothing."

"Will he—do you think Mr. Berge will be all right?" one of the women asked, but no one even tried to answer her question.

Before Sven had run a hundred yards he realized that he would never reach the village. His first hope had been that he might keep ahead of the bear and get into one of the houses. At the end of a hundred yards, though, he knew that he was already losing ground, even though he was pumping every ounce of speed possible into his legs.

For a second or so he felt panic surging inside him. Then he saw something which gave him an idea. Some three hundred yards away there was a large outcrop of rock which formed the north side of this gentle slope. It was a favorite playground for the children of Mykines.

In the cities of most countries children have playgrounds provided with swings and seesaws, slides and climbing frames and sandpits. On

Mykines there were only natural amusements, and among them was this great rock.

Some time—so long ago that no one could remember—it had been split from top to bottom, probably during a period of severe frost. The split was slightly sickle-shaped, wide enough at both ends for a child to race into, but narrowing at the middle.

It had provided endless hours of amusement and thrills for the youngsters. The middle section was so narrow that it could only be passed by climbing up a few feet, or actually wriggling through an eight-foot-long tunnel which some adventurous boy had scooped out. Going through that tunnel had been a dare among the boys of Mykines for a long time.

Remembering that little tunnel half way through the split rock gave Sven new hope. He knew he could get through it, and he was sure the bear could not. If he could draw the bear into the crack, then leave him stranded for only a few minutes at the entrance of that short tunnel, he would be safe.

This new plan gave added speed to his feet. He swerved to the right and began the slightly uphill climb to the rock. To Sven it seemed like a symbol of life, an unexpected deliverance from danger.

Only when he was about twenty yards from the opening did Sven suddenly have an uneasy feeling that all was not going so well as he thought. He shot a quick glance over his shoulder and was horrified to see that the bear had cut down the distance between them by half. He was now no more than twenty yards behind.

Sudden new panic struck Sven as he rushed nearer the big crack in the rock. A moment ago it had promised a way out of trouble; now he realized that if he did go in, it would be to his death. The bear was too close. Sven would need a second or so when he reached the middle of the rock to drop flat and crawl into the tunnel. He would not have that time. Before he could wriggle to safety, a claw-armed forepaw would smash down on him and yank him back to his death.

All this passed through his mind in a second or so, and at the last moment he swerved and ran along the front of the huge weather-worn rock. There was a surprised *woof* from behind him, and he even gained a yard or so before the bear could change direction.

Frantically Sven sought to wring a little extra speed from his tired legs, but it could not last. His muscles were growing more and more leaden and his breath was giving out. A minute at the most would see the end of the chase.

Passing the western fringe of the rock, he started to rush down the slight incline. He was so exhausted that he had gone thirty yards before he realized he had run into a trap—and this time there seemed no way out. Directly ahead of him was one of the island's worst bogholes.

It lay in a natural rock saucer, as if some prehistoric giant had dug a hand into the rock and scooped it out. Gradually the hollow had filled with water from the slopes on three sides. Once it must have been a clean little tarn, but now it was a sinkhole of mud and weeds.

Some eighty yards across, it looked at first glance like a circular patch of rough ground, with its fringes guarded by masses of spiky reeds. But the rough ground was no more than a maze of tiny islets, composed of many years' accumulation of rotted vegetation lying among a wealth of rank water weeds. There were even occasional patches of color where tiny flowers had somehow found a hold.

The bog was a safe haven for sea birds, and popular with eider ducks, which nested here every spring and sometimes hatched out a second brood late in the year. No islander ever ventured into this morass, though, no matter how many eggs there were for the taking. The danger was too great.

A yard or so from the outer patches of reed the depth was already more than three feet, and the slow-moving, peaty-brown water could be stirred up into glutinous mud by tossing a large stone into it.

Even though Sven was aware of the bog's dangers, he dared not slacken speed. The last time he had looked over his shoulder he had caught a momentary glimpse of the bear's shaggy, creamy-colored body no more than a dozen yards behind him. He could even hear the labored breathing of his pursuer. His own breathing was becoming more and more painful. Each time he filled his lungs it felt as if he had drawn a red-hot file across his chest. He was very near the point of collapse when he reached the reeds which fringed the bog.

As he felt the ground go suddenly spongy beneath his feet he made a wild leap for the nearest of the tiny islets. They were sparser near the fringe, and the water channels were wider. In ordinary circumstances he would never have gained his objective, but terror gave spring to his weary muscles.

His right foot came down on the stiff, dark-green reeds, pressing scores of them flat under his sheepskin shoe. They gave him a little support, acting as a miniature raft on the soggy ground; but as he swung forward to give another leap for the next islet, his foot pressed through, and instead of springing off the little patch he swayed forward and went under the dark-brown water with a tremendous splash. At the very last moment his foot came out of the mud with a horrible, sucking squelch.

Behind him there was another even greater splash. Coming from a land where even in the height of the short summer the bogs were never more than a few inches deep, the bear didn't hesitate when he reached the first patch of spongy soil.

He simply ran on into the bog, planting one forefoot on a little islet only a few feet behind Sven. His great weight drove his paw right through, sinking it to his shoulder.

He threw a great column of muddy water many feet into the air, and his head went down into the ooze. This was something he had never known before, and his first reaction was to fight to the surface. As he drew out his right paw he had to press down with his other paws, and they, too, dug deep into the clinging mud.

Ahead of him by no more than five feet, Sven struggled to the surface to hear a titanic battle going on behind him. By sheer physical strength the polar bear was breaking free. Flailing madly with all four paws, he was churning the mud and the water until they were turning into a thick porridge which could not hold him.

He looked a fearsome sight, for he was covered, except for a patch on his back, with thin mud. His head dripped dark-brown watery slime, in the middle of which his pink tongue and white teeth showed. Behind them, blinking rapidly to keep them clear, his eyes seemed to glow red with rage and the lust to kill.

Sven reached out for a grip on the weeds growing on a little islet ahead. The first grab did no more than break off half a dozen of the dark-green, brittle stems. He heaved himself painfully forward another few inches, managed to get hold of a good handful and hauled himself along. Behind him the bear was making progress, too.

He was making a tremendous row, woofing and growling, splashing and occasionally coughing, as mud was thrown up into his open mouth. Yet there was something about his savage determination which compelled admiration. He had the will to win, and brute strength was beating the holding power of the mud.

Sven made another yard. He grabbed at one little islet, and only succeeded in pulling it toward him: it was a floating patch of mud, held together by reed roots.

Foot by foot beast and boy fought their way nearer the center of the bog. Sven was as covered with mud as the bear, but he had the advantage of knowing how to use the tiny patches of semisolid land. The runnels in between were narrowing now, and the water was choked with aquatic growth, some of it so thick that twice Sven thought he would not get free when a foot became entangled.

The bear was not looking for islands. He was ploughing along by sheer strength, like some miniature icebreaker smashing its way through frozen seas by virtue of weight and massive horsepower. And he was winning.

Like an exhausted runner Sven could only get enough breath now by keeping his mouth wide open. His chest was heaving jerkily. There were spots and flashes of light coming and going in front of his eyes. In a curious detached way he realized that any moment now he would collapse.

He wanted to do just one thing—stand erect on one of the little hummocks which thrust upward from the sea of almost liquid mud, and then leap to the next. He felt if he could only get onto his feet, he might still win.

He reached a patch of reeds and coarse grass nearly a yard square and hauled himself almost onto it. His hands sank only a few inches into the muddy earth, but he could not heave himself out of the liquid mud. His legs felt as if great masses of iron were tied to them.

Slowly he allowed himself to sink chest down on the reeds, turning his head to one side so that he could still get the air he needed so badly. As if from a great distance he heard the polar bear threshing and splashing his way nearer, yet now Sven was no longer afraid. He had tried, he had done everything he could.

He closed his eyes. From somewhere very near he heard a tremendous splash. Instinctively he clasped his hands across the back of his neck, and waited for the crushing blow.

12: Unexpected Ally

As Sven sank into a half-conscious daze, so near to fainting that he was no longer afraid, the polar bear was growing exhausted. His thick fur was completely covered with heavy slime, and the sheer weight of it was telling on his tired muscles. He heaved himself onto what looked like solid ground, but it was no more than a floating patch of reeds and weeds, held together by mud.

As the bear flopped half onto it, the island capsized. It dropped the bear into the soft mud below, and turned over on top of him. For a minute the islet bobbed and heaved as a desperate battle for life went on beneath it. Then a mud-covered paw broke surface, and a few seconds later the bear's head and shoulders emerged.

Somehow, weary and exhausted though he was, the polar bear found the strength to fight his way to another patch of weeds and reeds. He swam close by Sven, so close that he could have scooped the boy into the mud with one stroke of his right paw. But he did not even look at him.

Like Sven, he was seeing through a red mist. The strength was fading from his mighty muscles. The past few hours' roaming about the island, and now this exhausting battle with the mud, had beaten him.

He stroked slowly, ponderously, through the mud, and laid a paw on the second islet. This one was solid. Panting hard he held onto it until he found the strength to raise himself up. Then, as Sven had done, he collapsed, to lie like an inert mass of mud, his eyes closed, his mouth open, his flanks heaving as he sought air, and more air.

Only a few minutes later Napoleon Berge arrived, calling Sven by name and looking anxiously in every direction. The women had seen boy and bear arrive at this spot; but now there was nothing to see except mud. Neither Sven nor the bear responded to the old man's anxiety-filled shouts. Both were sunk in a semicoma of complete exhaustion, and both were perfectly camouflaged by the mud.

The old man turned away, and stood for a few moments staring sadly up the slopes. Had Sven somehow managed to skirt the bog and get onto higher ground? He started to walk around the fringe of rushes, and it was then that something unusual caught his eye. It was only a little thing, but significant.

For many years a small colony of eider ducks had used this bog for nesting, and the "aw-aw-aw" of the drake was a never-ending music at mating time. Now—and it drew the old man's attention—an eider duck swept in toward the center of the bog, flapped its wings as if about to come down, only to winnow upward in sudden fright.

Napoleon stopped. It was not common for eiders to be here at this time of the year, but sometimes, if a hatch of eggs had met with an accident, the birds would brood a second lot of chicks.

Sitting down on a stone Napoleon watched the duck circle again, crying plaintively. That told him she was in trouble. Either her mate was hurt or she had young down there and was afraid to go to them.

After a few minutes the eider duck swung in once more. Her wings flapped furiously as she came down to land, but again at the very last moment she lifted into the air again.

Napoleon shaded his eyes, trying to see what it was that alarmed the duck. If there was something, it was well hidden—yet what could it be? There were no wild animals on Mykines, neither stoat nor weasel—not even rats. Slowly, methodically, Napoleon studied the area where the eider duck had twice tried to alight. There seemed no reason at all why the duck should be afraid to come down, but the old man continued to stare searchingly. Wild birds seldom made a mistake about dangers. There must be something there.

Finally he spotted it. Two mounds of mud—different from other mud patches in one small respect: there were no reeds or plants of any kind growing out of them. Napoleon studied the little mud patches from various points on the fringe of the bog, and finally decided that beneath them lay Sven and the bear.

His heart was beating wildly from anxiety when he finally got back to the houses. Aksel and the women who had been at East Cliff were there, busy gathering more food, dry clothes, and blankets. They looked anxiously at the old man, then at Maria Klakk. No one had yet found the courage to tell her about Sven.

"Have you left Sven on the cliff top?" Maria asked.

"They haven't told you?" Napoleon replied, shooting a swift glance at Aksel.

"Told me!" Maria said, suddenly fearful. "Why —what's happened? He's—"

"He saved us," Napoleon interrupted, trying to keep his voice steady. "He drew the bear away when our torches went out. He's in the Arnafjall bog—with the bear."

"Dead!" Maria whispered. "He is dead! I can feel it!"

"Rubbish!" Because Napoleon was so anxious his voice was unnecessarily harsh. "He may be dead—but I think he will be alive. He is yards from the bear. Now, you can help me. I want a good long plank, and we'll need ropes."

"Perhaps I had better come with you," Aksel suggested. "The women can—"

"There are men at East Cliff waiting for dry clothes and food," Napoleon said curtly. "We know *they* are alive. Keep them alive. I'll see to Sven."

The sun was touching the far horizon when Maria Klakk finally got to her son. The day which had begun so desperately, with howling winds and tempestuous seas, now had an unearthly quiet about it. There was no wind and the seas were going down very rapidly. Out here in the bog there was a quiet which frightened Maria. She had spent almost forty minutes working her way across the patches of mud and water, using two long planks to span the islets.

She was soaked to the waist, for like the polar bear she had encountered several small floating islets which had tipped under the weight of the plank and thrown her into the muddy water.

When she reached the bear she could find no sign of life at first. Then as she stared she detected a faint up-and-down movement of the mud-covered body. Sunk in the depths of exhaustion he was breathing like a child, slowly and evenly. Maria lifted a hand to the shotgun across her shoulders. She would never have another chance as good as this to kill the strange intruder on their island.

Her anxiety for Sven saved the bear. She could not spare the minute or so necessary to bridge the gap between her and the animal. Quietly she lifted her second plank and dropped an end close to Sven. A few moments later she was on her knees beside him, turning him slowly onto his back and patting his mud-caked cheeks.

It took some minutes to wake him and convince him that he was safe. Then came the task of getting out of the bog. They forgot the bear; both of them were desperately anxious to reach safety before darkness shrouded them.

When Sven, supported by his mother, finally stepped out onto solid ground once more, Napoleon hugged him in a grip which hurt. The old man did not speak. In those moments words were not easy to find.

As the three of them walked home, the skies were darkening and the first stars showing in a heaven almost clear of cloud. They could even see the pale beam of the Mykinesholmur light as it swept steadily round and round.

There were lights in the houses throughout the

night, for people were coming and going all during the dark hours. Women trudged the four miles to East Cliff with their driest peat blocks so the shipwrecked men could have an unfailing supply of fuel to keep their fires going. Wardrobes had been ransacked to ensure that every one of the schooner's crew would have dry clothing.

Edvin Christiansen had come down himself to tell them that next morning a motor boat would leave Thorshavn bringing a doctor, and also bringing a man with a heavy rifle, so the injured engineer would have immediate attention, and the polar bear could be dispatched.

The seas were smoothing off rapidly, and an hour after dawn Sven was wakened by his grandfather and told that the interisland boat was coming in, as well as the fleet of island boats which had gone off so bravely four days earlier to follow the school of whales.

Everyone from the village gathered at the foot of the boat landing. It hardly seemed possible that twenty-four hours earlier this sloping rock face up which the boats were hauled had been hidden by angry waves. Now there was only a slight swell breaking on the rocky slabs which made this approach so dangerous.

Sven stood with his Uncle Aksel and his grandfather and watched a dinghy put off from the interisland boat. Beyond that craft the Mykines boats, eleven in all, stood off. They were loaded to the gunwale with whale meat and blubber. Beyond, and coming up with a curl of white at her bows, was the motor boat bringing a doctor and a gunner from Thorshavn.

There was no sound as the dinghy bearing the first of the shipwrecked crew came closer. A bird winged overhead and squawked as if wondering what was going on.

Then the crew began to sing. With only the splash of quietly dipping oars as a background noise the voices rang out deep and reverent. It was a hymn of thanks.

On shore there was a breathless silence until the men stepped from the boat; the wives clasped husbands, mothers embraced sons, while children and neighbors stood by bright-eyed but silent.

Later in the morning boats arrived from Thorshavn with men to salvage the schooner's cargo of dried cod, and, if possible, patch up the battered hull and refloat the *Faroes Seeker* before the next storm.

Ashore, after a good meal and a rest, Sven's father went along with his son, Aksel and Napoleon, and the Thorshavn gunner to the bog. Several of the teen-age boys, who had returned from the whaling expedition to Vagar, had been up to the bog to see if the bear was still alive, and had reported that he was.

There were plenty of spectators to see the end of the drama. They had chattered cheerfully enough during the walk, but when they came to the bog silence fell over them all. The bear was squatting on his little island, trying vainly to rid himself of the caked mud which completely hid his creamy fur. He looked pathetic, and was obviously very weak.

"I don't think we'll have much difficulty here," the man with the rifle said, and walked around the bog to find the best shooting position.

Sven experienced a strange sense of horror as he looked at his enemy of yesterday. Then he would have shot the bear gladly. Now, remembering how the crew of the schooner had been almost miraculously saved, he suddenly felt sorry for the animal. It seemed unjust that he should be killed from a distance, with no chance to fight for his life.

Turning to his father, his face very grave, Sven asked, "Need he be killed? We—we have been so lucky. No lives lost, and—"

As if he had been waiting for the suggestion, Sven's father called to the gunner and told him not to shoot—for the time being. Only when they returned to the village, trying to think of some way to get the polar bear back into a cage, did an unexpected friend turn up. It was the doctor who had come to give what aid might be needed. He had done all he could for the injured engineer, and attended to the many cuts and bruises among the rest of the crew. Now he was waiting to return to Thorshavn.

He had the answer as to how the bear could be dealt with. A rough duckboard track was made, and across this the doctor walked until he was within a dozen feet of the bear. Behind him, in case of emergency, stood the man with the rifle.

The doctor's tool was simple—the rod from a fowling net, with a pad of cotton wool fastened to the end.

The bear turned to stare at the men, but made no move to get at them. The days of starvation had sapped his strength, and the final struggle in the bog had taken the last of his energy.

From a small bottle the doctor poured chloroform onto the cotton wool, then pushed the fifteen-foot rod across and held the anesthetic under the bear's nose.

The bear drew back, and for a moment it seemed as if the ruse would fail. But when the pad was thrust forward again the chloroform seemed to act swiftly. Within five minutes the mud-stained form was inert.

Once again the women of the village were called out to help as the 1,000-pound polar bear was slid and pulled across the bog. With the doctor giving more chloroform each time the bear showed signs of returning consciousness, the work of making a cage for him went on feverishly.

No one begrudged the sheep which went to feed their patient in the days which followed. Sven's father and Captain Neilsen had pointed out that if the creature could be got to Denmark in good shape, he might well be sold for between fourteen thousand and sixteen thousand kroner, and the money was to be equally divided among the crew of the *Faroes Seeker*.

When the animal was finally put aboard a boat for Thorshavn, looking much more himself—many gallons of water having cleaned off the clinging mud—Sven Klakk was not there to see him. He was up on the cliffs half a mile from the boat landing. With him was his Uncle Aksel.

Sven had persuaded Aksel to let him try his hand at netting sea birds, and his uncle had brought out his own *fleyg*, the same long-handled netting instrument with which years ago he had broken all records for fowling.

It was against the unwritten rules of the island, for Sven was still only sixteen, but he had persuaded Aksel to come with him, pleading that he had been old enough to go over the cliffs in bad weather—not once but twice—and he ought to have at least a chance to show his fowling skill.

After the recent bad weather the sea birds seemed busier than ever. They sailed down from the ledges to the blue-green of the water below, and beat their way back later on fast flickering wings. Sven had planted half a dozen stuffed guillemots on ledges near where he was crouched, and with a rope about his waist held by his uncle some thirty feet above him, he waited like a runner about to start an important race.

Down below the interisland boat moved off, a patch of white water at her stern, a dot of white on her foredeck . . . the polar bear in his cage.

Just then a puffin beat his way up from the sea, short sturdy wings winnowing in the cool air. His parrot beak had the red sheen of health on it. The bird swung along the cliff face, and if he saw Sven, no warning bell sounded in his small head. A moment later the long-handled *fleyg* swung smoothly out.

On the cliff above, Aksel Berge's eyebrows lifted and a little smile came over his leathery face. As a needle is drawn to a powerful magnet, so the puffin seemed to be drawn into the net. Aksel's keen ears actually caught the grunt as the bird struck the mesh.

He looked over, to watch with a professional eye as his nephew dipped a hand into the net and grabbed the struggling sea bird.

"His first bird, eh," Aksel said to himself. "I'll claim it for my supper—since I taught Sven how to swing the *fleyg*." Then the smile faded and was replaced with a puzzled frown.

Instead of wringing the puffin's neck, and slipping the dead bird into his belt, Sven held it for a few seconds, then tossed it into the air. There was a momentary flutter of wings as the little bird got his balance, then he was off, startled, frightened, but still alive.

Sven gave a tug on the rope to signal his uncle that he was coming up. Aksel took in the slack as his nephew climbed, heaving himself surely from ledge to ledge until he was safe on top.

"Why did you let it go?" Aksel asked.

For a moment Sven did not answer. Then, grinning a little sheepishly, he said:

"I don't know, Uncle Aksel. He was the very first bird I've netted. I—I suppose I'll have to get used to the idea that if a bird gets away, it's valuable food lost. But I just couldn't kill him. I guess I must be softhearted. We have been so lucky, haven't we? I just—well, I let him go as his share of the good luck."

Aksel nodded and smiled. He thought he understood. Out here where the wild Atlantic beat itself to foam against the cliffs, where even the bravest must quail at times in the fury of a storm, a man needed luck.

Side by side Sven and Aksel watched the interisland boat beating its way southeast. In less than three hours it would be entering the harbor at Thorshavn. There would probably be a crowd of people waiting, anxious to catch a glimpse of the big, cream-colored polar bear. Yet things might have been so different.

Sven and his Uncle Aksel must have been thinking the same thoughts, for as they turned to walk back toward the houses both said, almost in the same breath:

"We were lucky!"